Unforgivable

Mary L. Johnson

Dedication

To Beau

For his constant encouragement,
without which this book
would not have been written.

And to

Brenna & Josef,
Kyle & Allie,
Alex & Alexandra

For their love and support,
especially through a couple of
medical emergencies of my own.

Prologue

Back From the Dead

Present

Opening my eyes, I see the most beautiful sight in the world — my kids and husband walking into the room. They should seem happy to see me. They don't. Something's wrong. They look scared. My brain struggles. Thoughts slug to the surface like bubbles in hot August tar. Thick. Slow.

Where am I? I look around. I'm in a hospital room.

Why?

Zoe, Christopher, and Michael creep to my bed, as if afraid of breaking me. They crowd in close to touch me. Smiles don't mask the worry in their eyes.

"It's okay, Sheena," Michael says. Strain cracks his normally calm voice. "You're going to be okay." He strokes my hand, the one with a little plastic thing snapped to the *finger.*

The other side has an IV attached. Zoe's hand softly covers the tape.

"What happened?" My voice sounds croaky, weak. Every part of me hurts.

My mind frantically searches its memory banks. Empty. Zilch. A blank nothingness, giant and black. A void waiting to draw me back down into it.

Palpable fear radiates off my family.

Christopher lays a hand on my leg. "You were in a car accident, Mom."

"The people in the other car are okay," Michael answers the question before my sluggish brain forms it.

I study their faces, desperate for reassurance. None of them meet my gaze. They stare at something behind me that beeps. A monitor? Zoe's eyes are nearly swollen shut from crying. I can't remember ever seeing her look this devastated.

Can I? My mind, always so sharp and reliable, fails me. Panic presses down on me, far heavier than the cotton hospital blanket.

"What happened?"

"Not now, Sheena," Michael says, his take-charge tone back.

A nurse who's been hovering in the background steps forward.

"That's right, Mrs. McKenzie. You need to rest. The doctors worked hard to keep you alive. Let's not hinder their efforts."

"Alive?"

Michael grips down on my hand. "CareFlite brought you here. They revived you three times."

"I died?" Why can't I remember any of this?

Zoe sobs and turns around, lurching for the tissues on the counter. My husband shrugs, looking stricken.

"Everyone's been praying, Mom." Hope flares in Christopher's nearly-adult face. "Everyone from your Bible study, the church, even people that read about the accident on social media and passed it on. People around the world we don't even know are praying."

The anxiety lifts. Everything will be okay.

A tawny lion, mane black and bristling, pads past in the hallway. Silent. Transparent. Glowing. The huge feline pauses at the door. I stare at him, and, somehow, he doesn't seem out of place. His inky black eyes look deep into mine.

This makes perfect sense, even though nothing else does.

Chapter One

Dance Team Tryouts

Three Months Earlier

"Pull over, Mom," Zoe screeched. "I'm going to be sick."

Glancing from her pale face to the rearview mirror, I steered the Mazda CX-5 to the curb. My fifteen-year-old daughter unlatched her seatbelt and bolted from the car. She stood, hands on knees, head hanging down, the curls of her long dark hair covering the front of her High Kicker's dance uniform.

Saturday morning traffic curled around us, streaming into the Dallas-Fort Worth Metroplex from our town on the outskirts. A minute ticked by while I watched her take deep breaths, letting her stomach settle down. My poor kiddo, so anxious about officer tryouts for her high school drill team.

"How do you feel?"

She straightened, her skin pale. "Better, I guess." Zoe climbed into the car again. "Sorry."

"That's okay, sweetie. I'm just glad you didn't toss your toast." I waited a beat, but obviously she wasn't in the mood for my goofy humor. "It's hard, but try not to worry ahead of time. I know you'll do great."

"You're my mom. You have to say that."

"True. It's in the Mom rulebook." That brought a hint of a smile. I grinned at her. "But that doesn't make me wrong."

She rolled her eyes and sighed as I pulled back into traffic.

"Why are you so nervous this year?" I asked. "I would have thought last year trying to get *on* the team would have been the hard part."

Zoe had dreamed of wearing the white sequined cowboy hat of a Kicker officer since she'd first seen the dance team three years ago. They'd performed at a pep rally while we watched her older brother, then a freshman, on the Honor Guard spirit team. The dancers' precision dance moves cheered on their school's sports teams, while the Honor Guard used zany antics to motivate the crowd.

"You know how it is, Mom. I've never been one of The Graitney Greats."

"Oh, Zoe, don't say that. You're an exceptional dancer, and you've been dancing as long or longer than any of them. You're a High Kicker now. Surely, that makes you part of the in-group."

Out of the corner of my eye, I saw her shaking her head. "You know that doesn't make me a Great."

She didn't have to explain. Every teenaged girl and her mom were aware of The Greats. A handful of kids whose parents spoiled them not only with cars, clothes, and things but with an exalted idea of where they belonged in the small universe of Graitney, Texas. Those kids and their wealthy parents were the sun. Everyone else simply spun in orbit around them.

Michael and I didn't have the money to lavish on our kids like some parents, even if we'd wanted to. Michael made a good salary as the Chief of Police that I supplemented with a jewelry making business. But it wasn't the kind of dough the seriously rich folks around here had.

Zoe's fists clenched tightly in her lap. I hurt for her.

We'd arrived at the school, and I jerked my thoughts back to the present, reminding myself I just needed to trust God with my kids. I said a little prayer for Zoe to do her best in the tryouts.

We parked in the lot near the gym and headed inside. The poor girls hadn't even danced yet, and the pungent scent of nervous sweat washed over us as we entered. The heels of Zoe's white Kicker cowboy boots clacked on the institutional-green linoleum, a brisk staccato.

The girls clumped together on one side of the hallway. The three senior officers – Greats, of course – stood in the middle. The parents clustered on the other side of the space.

I spotted my oldest friend, Tracy, amid the girls. The neon pink streaks at the tips of her long blonde hair were hard to miss. We'd gone to high school and college together. She owned the local dance studio. Many of the girls had been her pupils since they were toddlers. They clustered around her each getting a hug and a whispered word of encouragement. Zoe hurried over to join them.

"Hi, Sheena." My friend, Kara, slid up beside me. "Isn't this nerve-wracking? I don't think Emily slept all night."

Zoe and Emily had been besties since taking their first dance class at Tracy's studio when they were four. They'd attended the same church their entire lives. Both Kara's and my prayers had been answered last year when the two girls made the drill team together. We couldn't imagine what would have happened if only one of them had gotten on without the other.

Now, I wondered the same thing about their being made officers.

Kara's eyes scanned the gaggle of girls. "It looks like all forty-two girls who are sophomores and above are here. Can you believe only six will be chosen as officers?"

I couldn't help snorting. "Three are returning seniors. So, for all intents and purposes, there are only three slots for the younger girls."

"You're right." Kara's shoulders slumped. "I hadn't thought of that." She turned back toward me. "How's Zoe holding up?"

I sighed, and lowered my voice, not wanting other moms to overhear. "You know her nervous stomach. I had to pull over on the way here, but she managed not to up-chuck."

"Thank goodness for small blessings."

The low hum of conversation stopped immediately when Miss Williams, the drill team sponsor, raised her voice. "All right, ladies. It's time to begin."

She faced the cluster of anxious moms and a scattering of dads. "Parents, just to be clear about how this works, only the girls are allowed into the gym. Each candidate will perform the three-minute piece they've choreographed. Our panel of judges includes me and two other dance instructors from other schools. Our decision is final. I'll post the outcome on the drill team's webpage by five tonight. Parents may wait out here, but this will take several hours. I'm collecting the girls' cell phones, and I will return them when we're finished so they can call for rides."

With that, she ushered the girls into the gym. The first time I'd seen Miss Williams at last year's tryouts, I'd assumed she was one of the girls with her youthful face, smooth ebony skin, and bouncy ponytail. She had been a Kilgore College Rangerette herself and had told me she appreciated Zoe's dancing ability. I hoped she saw leadership potential in my daughter, as well. That was a separate ranking that only she gave the girls. It weighed as heavily as the dance portion.

"I don't know about you," Kara stared at the gym doors once they closed, "but I'm too anxious to go home."

Tracy heard her and walked over to us. "Want to grab coffee? If I remember correctly, last year's tryouts took four hours."

Four hours! I didn't know if I could manage to swallow coffee. My throat felt constricted like I had stage-fright myself, but doing anything seemed better than pulling up a folding chair and watching the gym door.

"Sure. Coffee sounds good."

Chapter Two

What's Real?

Present

I wake again and recognize a soft familiar snore. Michael sleeps in an armchair that pulls out into a tiny twin bed. His long legs stick awkwardly over the end. He must be miserable. Machines beep and hum. Something smells sharp. Astringent. Antiseptic. Tape pulls my skin where an IV pokes into a vein. It hurts. As do my head, arms, ribs, and leg. A nurse looks up from a desk right outside my room.

I'm in the ICU.

Michael sits up. Obviously, he wasn't sleeping well.

"Hey, there. How are you feeling?" he asks, rubbing a fist into one eye and yawning.

Looking at him, I see my grandparents just over his shoulder. The wall behind them is completely visible *through their translucent bodies. Papa, a Baptist preacher, and Nana, his wife of sixty years, are working in their garden. They chat amiably as they fill a wicker basket with produce.*

"I feel weird," I croak, my throat parched. "What time is it?"

Michael glances at his watch. "Ten after two." He runs a large hand over his face.

"At night?" There aren't any windows in the room.

He nods. I notice the scruff on his face has a sprinkling of silver among the black hairs. I didn't know that his beard was turning grey like his sideburns. He was a military policeman when we met, then a civilian cop. I've rarely seen him not clean-shaven.

As I stare at him, my grandparents vanish. They must have had something important to do. I can't remember if they told me what it was.

They've been dead for years.

I remember that I can't remember. There is a huge gap there. I can't recall much of anything. Even some common words are gone. I try to think through what happened.

Pictures flicker in my thoughts like old film. Flashes of nurses and doctors tending to me. Poking me. Taking blood. Family coming and going. It must be real, because I seem to be in the hospital. I still don't know how I got here.

I'm pretty sure I've asked, but no one will tell me.

Maybe Papa and Nana will when they come back

Chapter Three

Three Months Earlier

Tracy took her own car, but Kara and I drove together to Harvest Haven, located in what used to be a warehouse district near the railroad tracks. Volunteers from a local Christian-based addiction recovery ministry ran the popular coffee shop. All the proceeds supported the ministry. Soft praise music and the rich scent of coffee and pastries greeted us as I pushed open the door. The exposed brick walls covered with plants and uplifting scriptures made this one of the most pleasant places in town to meet.

We scanned the large room which held a variety of booths, tables and armchairs. People used the coffee shop for small Bible study groups or to meet with those they discipled. We waved through the window at Tracy, who was outside on the patio drinking a green smoothie.

Probably healthy and yucky. We queued up at the counter. I ordered a hazelnut latte, Kara a Speedy Gonzales, which is Mexican hot chocolate with two expresso shots.

We took our drinks outside to Tracy's table. A little breeze and the roof over the patio kept it cool.

"Emily seemed to be okay, but Zoe sure looked nervous," Tracy said after we got settled. "I think she's rather like her mom at that age. Anxious to fit in."

I nodded. "To say the least. There's been more than once that I wished she shared Christopher's personality. He doesn't stress about things. Just like Michael. But you're right Zoe's temperament is so much like mine. She worries too much about what people think."

I hoped that becoming an officer would help her feel accepted and maybe make her accept herself.

"Wanting to be popular is a normal teenage thing," Tracy assured me. "It can be rough."

Not with all teens. Christopher had morphed smoothly from childhood to adolescence into young adulthood. I never worried about him. Zoe was a good kid, too, but for some reason, I wanted to flash-freeze her in time. Perhaps because she was my youngest.

We chatted about how we thought the girls would do and which ones we thought would become officers. Tracy insisted both our girls should make it. She knew their dancing ability better than anyone, so I wanted to believe her, but part of me wondered if she was just being kind. She had a larger heart than most anyone I knew.

"You both must be so proud of your girls," she said. "It takes a lot of guts for them to put themselves out there like that. It's a lot of pressure and not all about their dancing ability."

"Well, they've had a great dance teacher," Kara said. "So, the technical part isn't an issue."

Tracy gave her a fleeting grateful smile, not her normal enormous one. "Anyone can teach dance. It's parents that give their children the confidence to soar."

I made a scoffing sound. "What are you talking about, Trace? You're their biggest cheerleader. You have done as much for our girls' confidence as anyone."

"I hope that's true." Her eyes looked sad. "It would be nice to think I've made a difference in someone's life."

"Oh, I'm sorry," Kara said, "We've been blabbing away without asking you about your divo—"

Tracy raised her voice over Kara's, "No problem. The divorce was finalized last week, and I've got to get used to my new reality."

Kara clucked sympathetically.

"I tried to make it work with Rod for way too long." Tracy shrugged. "It's just that I'd thought my life would be so different by this point."

"Kids," I said. "You've always joked that you wanted

a dozen kids."

This brought a grin paired with the sad eyes. Tracy chuckled without humor. An awkward silence fell.

Having children had been only one area of contention in their marriage, but Tracy had always kept her hopes up. Now newly divorced at forty-two, she would have to start all over with someone else. For her sake, I hoped she'd find that someone.

"Like we were just saying, God gave you a hundred kids to mother," I said, "and you do a terrific job."

"No, kidding," Kara added. "I don't know what all of us would do without you keeping our girls on track while they've grown up."

"We need all the help we can get," I said, putting down my mug. "Although, I'm thankful we have great kids who never really give us any trouble."

For a moment, Tracy's deep brown eyes caught and held mine. The teasing light was back. We'd gone through a bit of a wild time together, and I knew she caught the irony. Tracy winked, but Kara missed the joke. She was a newer addition to our friendship circle, and we'd never filled her in completely about our hard-partying college days.

I hurried to change the subject. "For some reason, these officer tryouts make me tense. It's like Zo's growing up too fast. One day she's starting high school just trying out to be a Kicker, and now she wants to be a team leader. I want to rewind the clock back to stuffed animals, tree forts, and pink tutus. Remember how adorable they were when they first started dancing?"

As if my words had conjured up reality, we all turned at the sound of a child shrieking.

"Mizz Tracy!" a little voice yelled.

A round-faced youngster with two bouncy ponytails high on her head toddled toward the table. She threw her arms around Tracy's legs in a tremendous hug. "I mithed you!"

"I missed you too, Angela." Tracy snaked an arm around the little girl's back and grinned up at the mom who had followed. "How are you, Casey? Is Jackson feeling better?"

"He's doing fine now, thanks." The young mother hiked an enormous purse higher on her shoulder. "Angela will be back in class tomorrow."

The little face tilted up toward Tracy beamed. "Tomowwow," she echoed.

"I'll see you then, sweetie." Tracy kissed the top of the child's head.

The mom grabbed the girl's hand and they left through the patio gate.

Tracy spoke in a low voice even though they couldn't have heard her. "My heart goes out to her. Casey's a single mom, raising two sweet kids on a waitress's tips. She's amazing."

I knew Tracy well enough to know she gave deep discounts on dance lessons to people who needed them. I glanced across the table at her. The light had returned to her face.

Chapter Four

Out Of Focus

Present

Coming to again, I haven't the faintest idea of the time. No thingy that tells the hour is in the room. I tug on an elusive memory. Clock. It's horrible struggling to think of simple words.

I can't get up because I'm strapped to all kinds of machines. An IV line runs out of my left arm. The liquid running in is cold. Sticky pads attach wires to my chest. A small clamp is still on the first finger of my other hand. There are burns on my arms. My left thigh has a bulky bandage. Some medical person said I'd lost a lot of blood through the jagged tear there.

Things come in and out of focus. I've never done illegal drugs, but I assume the way my mind jumps from image to *image and thought to thought is what a bad trip is like.*

Beeping noise – annoying.

Headache – better.

Lips – chapped.

At least, Tracy comes to visit. Just seeing her makes me smile. She always makes me laugh.

"Hospital gowns are the new black."

All the giggling wears me out. I sleep again.

Christopher swings so high I'm afraid he'll sail right out of the seat; his little legs pumping hard. Michael sings show tunes in the shower. Nana tells me stories about her childhood. I'm glad the people I love are here with me.

But Zoe cries a lot.

Chapter Five

Out Of The Frying Pan

Three Months Earlier

We dawdled over coffee, but Tracy left, heading for the studio to do some bookkeeping. Kara and I still got back to the high school too soon. We walked around the building a couple of times hoping to burn off the calories from the rich coffees. I glanced at my phone checking the temperature. It wasn't even noon yet, but the sun, intense and relentless, rocketed the late April temperature to nine-five degrees. We gave up and took refuge inside where it was cooler.

"I'd hate for The Blondes to see us sweating," I said running a hand over my wet forehead.

In general, we were too grown-up to have tacky nicknames like Graitney's Greats, but my friends and I thought of the town's female movers and shakers as The

Blondes. The three core women all wore a salon-created shade of gold hair and matching attitudes that let everyone else know just what golden lives they lived.

Growing up skinny, flat-chested, with black hair in the days of "blondes have more fun" didn't color my perspective, I'm sure. But even my blonde friends used the term. It fit so well.

"No kidding," Kara agreed, mopping her own forehead. "It's not as if we aren't sweating these tryouts already."

We'd no more than walked inside, faces flushed, shirts sticking to our damp skin, hair frizzing, than three of The Blondes descended on us.

Kimberly Malik – for some inexplicable reason known to her friends as Kuddles – was the leader of the group. She wore her hair in a platinum-white pixie cut, spiky on top. It neatly matched the Texas-sized rhinestone cross she wore around her neck. A tall woman, Kuddles towered over her shorter husband who was a partner in a leading law firm in Dallas. I'm tall at five-foot-nine, but she had a couple of inches on me.

Despite her dark eyes and coloring, Aimée Alterman's medium length, perfectly-tousled hair had been professionally colored to a glowing, honey shade. Her husband was supposed to be a bigwig in the finance world. Not something I could personally verify. It wasn't a world

Michael and I knew anything about.

The third woman, Jennifer Duran, probably didn't really qualify as a blonde. Her long dark hair had multiple highlights, in every shade of the color, as if trying to fit in with her friends. She stood quietly, hands clasped. Her normal disposition. I'd heard she and her husband made their money with a string of dry cleaners in Dallas and Fort Worth. Not the most glamorous occupation. She always seemed thrilled simply to be included in the power circle.

"We don't know anything yet, of course," Kuddles said to us, with a titter of fake humility, "but we have a good idea of who next year's officers will be."

All three of their girls were returning senior officers. One of them would have to commit murder over the summer to not retain the position.

As she usually did, Aimée Alterman continued her friend's thoughts, "So we are talking to the mothers of the most likely new officers."

"If one of your girls makes the cut," Kuddles said this with a tone that clearly implied it would be a momentous achievement, "we need to immediately start planning for summer camp."

Aimée added, "It will be here before we know it, so we drew up some preliminary plans this spring."

"Good thinking," Kara said with a straight face. "We'd be hard pressed to get the girls ready for camp with only two months' notice."

Her sarcasm went right over The Blondes' heads.

"Well, right. One can't leave such important matters until the last minute." Kuddles straightened herself up, clearly finished delivering the message.

"If Zoe and Emily are fortunate enough to be chosen as officers," I held Kuddles's gaze, trying to look as if I wasn't the least intimidated, "we look forward to working with you."

"Liar," Kara whispered as soon as the three were out of earshot.

We looked at each other, opening our eyes wide in an effort not to roll them.

"Those ladies make me feel like a teenager who isn't part of the cool group all over again."

"No kidding," I agreed. "I get mad at myself every time I let them get to me, since I wouldn't want to be a part of their group anyway. How nuts is that?"

We watched The Blondes as they worked their way around the hallway talking to the mothers of those girls they thought had a chance to be officers.

"As if it isn't bad enough that they set themselves up as the reigning queen bees," I added, "it's just downright mean to be talking to moms about what the officers will be doing this summer, when most of their daughters won't make the cut."

"You're right. How awful can they get?"

Another hour trudged by before the gym door opened, and the Kickers started coming out. We'd been talking to the other non-Blonde moms. All eyes turned toward the girls. The daughters of The Blondes, Layla Malik, Madison Alterman, and Isabella Duran, younger nearly mirror-images of their mothers without the bottle-bleached hair, came out first looking supremely confident. The rest of the team trailed behind. Some girls appeared crushed, clearly holding back tears. I took that to mean their pieces hadn't gone well. A few of the team members seemed cautiously optimistic.

Zoe and Emily walked out together, the last ones to leave. I scanned their faces trying to decipher their moods. Kara's daughter had a spark of excitement in her round brown eyes. Her strawberry-blonde hair looked as if she'd been running her hands through it. She had a sweet, quiet disposition, and although both girls were pretty, it seemed to me that Emily's confidence ran deeper than Zoe's.

My daughter's face looked stony. She was working hard to keep herself in check.

Had something gone wrong? I'd watched Zoe practice her piece over and over. She danced flawlessly.

The girls said goodbye to their friends while we wished the other moms good luck. Outside, Emily and Kara gave each other a hug before parting.

"So, how did it go?" I asked as soon as the car doors shut.

Tears pooled in Zoe's eyes. "My grand jeté wasn't nearly as high as in practice, and I wobbled at the end of my pirouette."

I tried not to snort. She seemed to float during the split-like leap and there wasn't a girl on the team who could spin like my daughter. Why was she always so hard on herself?

"Sweetie, some of the other girls don't have a ballet or jazz background at all, and you have both. You don't seem to even touch the floor when you dance. I'm sure your number went great."

I started the car. "Besides, you have the best high kick on the whole team." It didn't hurt that she had unusually long legs for her slim five-foot, seven-inch frame. "Your team's called *High Kickers*, remember?"

Zoe, who was a good student, did this after every exam, too. It was as if expecting the worst, she wouldn't be disappointed when it came. I hated it, but I kind of got it, as well. I'd done the same thing as a teen.

I reached over and patted her leg. "No matter what happens, I'm proud of you for trying out. That took a lot of nerve."

She dashed a hand across her cheek and managed a smile. "You always say you're proud of me."

"That's because I always am."

"Miss Tracy says so, too. No offense, Mom, but when it comes to dance, I take her word for it a little more than yours. She's got really high standards, and she makes us earn every advancement."

Tracy had taught Zoe so much about hard work and discipline, as well as a deep love of the art of dancing. I owed her a lot.

Just mentioning Tracy, seemed to have calmed Zoe down.

"At least, my layout was good," she said, talking about a kick where the dancer arches gracefully all the way back while kicking one leg straight up in the air.

Once the dam had broken, she launched into describing what the other girls did. "Haley tried to do this hip-hop thing, but she isn't built for it at all. Paige did tap, of course. It was good. Emily was awesome. Big surprise there."

She talked all the way home, but her nerves returned when I swung into our neighborhood. We lived in a two-story home in an older neighborhood of custom houses buried in oak trees. Michael had a thing against the McMansions The Blondes had snapped up on the edge of town.

"They are cookie-cutter homes," he said when the colossal luxury houses first went up. "Every sixth one is the exact same."

"Yeah, I'd *hate* to have to clean seven or eight thousand square feet," I'd answered, only half joking. The homes were gorgeous. If you could afford one, you could afford to have it cleaned.

We went into the house and Zoe showered while I made lunch. Our breakfast nook looked out over the pool and the yard Michael lovingly maintained. He said he couldn't live in Texas during the summer without a pool. It had been a boon with the kids, because we decided long ago to be the house where our children's friends wanted to hang out. During the summer, we often had a bunch of kids swimming. We kept that up as they'd gotten older. Especially with their buddies from church.

Some of the school friends not so much.

"Being popular in high school has a lot to do with who throws and attends the best parties," Christopher explained to us when a couple of his friends quit coming around once they hit high school. "It isn't as if we'll be invited to those kinds of parties. Dad isn't just a cop. He's the *top* cop."

As I sliced our sandwiches, I wondered if Michael's job had something to do with Zoe's intense desire to fit in. Does she see her dad as a hindrance to being cool? Like so many people I spent my teen years with no clue how to be a part of the right group.

Michael swung by on his lunch break to tell her he was rooting for her.

"How did she do, She-Girl?" he asked grabbing one of the brownies I'd baked.

When we'd first started dating seriously, he began calling me "his girl," eventually it morphed with my name Sheena into "She-Girl," which he'd called me ever since.

"Oh, you know how she obsesses over the tiniest flaw, but it sounded to me as if she gave her normal wonderful performance."

The delight on his face was as warm and rich as the brownie he held. Zoe came into the kitchen her hair hanging down her back in long wet curls. She had the best hair, but, of course, much of the time she straightened it to look like the other girls.

"Mom told me you did great, Kiddo." Michael said as she walked in. "You'll be wearing that sequined hat for sure."

"Thanks, Dad." Zoe gave him a hug. "I don't know what I'll do if I don't make it."

My six-foot, two-inch husband backed away and looked down at her suddenly serious, his brownie-free hand resting on her shoulder. "You'll pull yourself up by those white cowboy boots and get on with life. That's what we McKenzies do. You know that."

She straightened her back. "You're right, Dad. I do."

I could have rushed across the room and kissed him right on his chocolate-covered lips. Why could I never think of the right thing to say?

After Michael went back to work, it was just the two of us in the house. Christopher had wrangled time off work at a local restaurant to go to Six Flags with his friends. It was one of the first nice Saturdays before summer break when the park would get packed.

We watched *American in Paris*, which had been one of Zoe's favorite movies for years, but it didn't hold her attention. She watched with one eye on the clock the other on her phone as she texted her friends. Our two Ragdoll cats, Anne and Andy, curled up on the couch with us. Michael had saved them from an illegal breeder nearly a year ago. At the time, the two kittens had been so tiny and sick that the rescue facility that took the rest of the expensive cats wouldn't touch them. Zoe nursed the two babies by hand, getting up every three hours at night to feed them. Andy, the beautiful white and chocolate male, worshipped her still. Over time, Anne, with her distinct white and silver coloring, became more attached to me. I understood the value of kitty treats.

As it got closer to five o'clock, the hour of the drill team sponsor's posting, my stomach balled into a tighter knot than the one in the laces of my running shoes. I had my MacBook Air on the couch with the school website pulled up and open to the dance troupe's page. Zoe was doing the same on her iPad. At a quarter to the hour, I saw her refresh the page. I did too.

Finally, up popped a list of the next school year's officers: Captain, Layla Malik; Lt. Captain, Isabella Duran; Sr. Lieutenant, Madison Alterman. That accounted for the returning seniors, all Greats.

I wondered what Aimée Alterman thought of the quiet Jennifer Duran's daughter ranking higher than her own? Would that cause tension in the Golden ranks?

Continuing down the list I read, Sr. Lieutenant, Paige Turner. What in the world were her parent's thinking giving that poor girl such a name?

Jr. Lieutenant, Zoe McKenzie. Jr. Lieutenant, Emily Webb.

Zoe and Emily! My breathing froze while I reread the last two names to double check. I needn't have bothered.

Zoe's happy yell filled the air. "I did it! We did it! Em and I made it!"

She'd leapt off the couch and danced around the room. I jumped up and pulled her into a hug, blinking back tears. I was so happy for her and doubly happy that both she and Emily had made officer rank.

Before we'd broken apart, her phone started dinging with texts.

"It's Christopher," she said, laughing. "I can't believe he congratulated me before Emily did."

"I can't believe your brother's paying attention to the

results from Six Flags."

"And Daddy," she said, her lips breaking into the largest smile I'd seen on her in days. "Miss Tracy sent me congratulations, too."

Then her phone rang. Rather unusual as the kids mostly texted.

She punched it on. "Hi, Em. Can you believe it? We both made it."

Zoe ran upstairs to her bedroom to talk. Andy bounded after her as if it were a game of chase. My own phone chimed, and I answered, assuming it was Kara.

A totally different voice answered my greeting. "This is Kimberly Malik. We have a meeting of Kicker mothers scheduled for next Monday evening at my house. We officer mothers are bringing the food. I've put you down for kale salad and croissants."

Chapter Six

What Does That Mean?

Present

Seems like I should be getting better, but I can't concentrate on anything. Can't direct my thoughts.

Clipboard on the counter. Water spot on the ceiling. Memories of last year's vacation to Disney World. I love Pirates of the Caribbean.

Two men talk outside my door. Maybe that's what woke me.

My eyes zoom in on the taller guy's lips, watching closely. Dialogue bubbles balloon above the two men's heads. The words scroll by like in a cartoon.

"...because of the accident," he says.

My accident?

"The Sheriff's office is waiting on the toxic screening,"

says the other man. "That had to be sent to the state lab."

Was the other driver drunk? High?

They said something I couldn't make out. Then I caught my name.

"Mrs. McKenzie's results amaze me. Really amaze me. I expected traumatic brain injury, but her MRI and CT are essentially normal. No damage."

"Well, I'm still concerned about the hypotension and hypoxemia. No idea what to make of them."

"Results perhaps of the dehydration?"

The words make no sense, but they mesmerize me.

A dictionary floats in front of my eyes. I remember the summer when Tracy and I raced to see who could read the whole thing first. That was back when she was still nerdy, before she discovered dance. Then she became popular, but she stayed my friend.

"She's lost a lot of blood. We assumed from that leg wound, although, now, that doesn't seem to be the culprit. The event appears to be multifactorial in etiology at this point. I'd be reluctant to release her without knowing the cause."

I have no idea what the words he just said mean.

They hurt my brain.

Chapter Seven

A Warning

Three Months Earlier

A couple of days later, Zoe still hadn't come down from the high of making Jr. Lieutenant. Even Michael with his hectic schedule noticed.

"I'm glad Zoe and Christopher are busy with all their various activities," he said after dinner Monday evening. "Too much free time can lead teenagers to do stupid things."

I'd been putting away leftovers, but I paused and glanced over at him where he was loading dishes into the dishwasher. Behind him, hummingbirds took turns outside the bay window, swooping into the red feeder, happy for their supper.

"Something in particular worrying you?"

He shrugged and concentrated on rinsing a plate.

I tried a different tactic. "What kind of stupid stuff?"

"You know, teen stuff." He dried his hands and came over and gave me a kiss on the top of the head. "Have fun with The Blondes tonight. I've got to run into work. There's some paperwork I need to catch up on."

Our first meeting with The Blondes, now that Emily and Zoe were officers, wasn't exactly something Kara and I would call fun. We gutted it out, but the moment the doors to Kara's minivan closed on our way home, she let loose.

"'Be aware that as High Kicker officers your daughters, and needless to say, their mothers have a certain standard to uphold,'" mimicked Kara in an almost perfect impression of Kuddles Malik's bossy twang. "A certain standard to uphold! Jeesh! What does she think we're going to do, run naked through the streets or something? Don't they know your husband's the Chief of Police and Eric publishes the town's newspaper? As if either of us or our kids would do something embarrassing."

She continued in a nasty tone unusual from my sweet friend. "If the rumors I've heard about her precious Layla's older brother Logan are true, I'll eat my...."

I glanced over because she'd stopped talking, her eyes firmly on the road.

"Yes?"

It didn't take much prodding.

"Oh, you remember there was that group of kids who

were busted for minors in possession last year. Kuddles' hotshot lawyer husband got the whole thing hushed up somehow. I bet you know all the juicy details."

I remembered hearing about it from another cop's wife. For a few weeks, it had been quite the buzz about town. However, Michael and I had a pact that nothing he shared about work ever left the two of us. Not even to my best friend.

Especially not to my best friend!

As publisher of the *Graitney Gazette*, Kara's husband, Eric, might not make all the day-to-day decisions on each story, but he had the final say. The business had been in his family since the town's founding. Michael liked to say Eric potty-trained on newsprint. Even in these tough times for print media, Eric kept the paper solvent. Graitney with a little over thirty thousand people had been one of the first in the Dallas-Fort Worth area to offer its newspaper online. He had great business savvy, but in his heart, he was a newsman. Michael warned me long ago to always keep that in mind when talking to Kara.

"Anyway," she said in a kinder tone, now, "I don't gossip, but just because they wear big crosses, doesn't make them super-saints. I just can't believe the nerve of those women."

"They are probably trying to watch out for the reputation of the entire team."

"Oh, Sheena, I love you, but do you always have to see the best in people?" She laughed. "Especially, when I want to rant."

I needed to talk about something else. Besides already feeling sensitive about not meeting The Blondes' standards, I'm a typical momma bear. Attack my child and I'll attack back. I didn't want to let my thoughts dwell on their telling us and our kids how to behave. It would only tick me off, and I wanted to be happy for Zoe and Emily's accomplishment.

"I *did* like getting to see the inside of Kuddles' house." I said. "I've been dying to for ages. I think my entire house would fit inside her kitchen and family room."

"No kidding. I'm so jealous. Two spiral staircases. A gigantic media room, and a wine cellar. Jeesh!"

Kara and I talked about Kuddles' fancy house all the way back to our neighborhood. We decided her outdoor kitchen had nicer appliances than our indoor ones. Not that I'd trade. My sunny, spacious kitchen was one of my favorite things about our house.

"There's one thing we've got that The Blondes' money can't buy," Kara said smugly as she swung into my driveway.

"What's that?"

"Mature trees. The best part of living on this end of town. Their fancy-schmancy subdivision was cut out of a hay field. It will be thirty years before their yards look this gorgeous."

Our yard glowed at night. Michael believed in landscape lighting for extra security. Every tree, shrub and walkway around our house shown with artfully placed streams of light. I spotted Anne or Andy's plummy tail disappearing behind a pink-flowering azalea bush.

She chuckled. "I overheard Aimée saying something to Heather about it. How cool that we've got something The Blondes envy."

A spotlight lit up the keypad on the garage door. It shone in Kara's laughing eyes and struck golden highlights in her strawberry blonde hair. She and Emily, like Zoe and I, had the same coloring. Like mother like daughter.

She'd been the first one of our group to call the haughty clique of female adults "The Blondes" when we met them just as the girls started middle school.

I'd questioned it, since Kara and her daughter were so fair, too.

"Yeah, but our hair color doesn't come out of a bottle," she'd said. "Well, okay, Em's doesn't." She'd fluffed her hair, self-consciously. "At least mine used to be this color naturally. Besides, it fits them. They give the rest of us a bad name."

Tracy, also a blonde, got a kick out of it, too, and the nickname stuck.

"It's almost eleven," Kara said suddenly, looking at the clock on the dash. "I've got yoga in the morning. You've got to try it."

A new combination yoga studio, health bar, and auto repair shop just opened. That's Graitney, Texas. Close enough to the city to try and be sophisticated. Small enough to be practical. Get healthy while having the oil changed.

"I'm thinking about it, but I like getting my run in before it gets too hot." I reached into the folder Aimée Alterman had given me. "Here's your list of businesses to solicit donations from for summer camp and ads for the football program."

"I bet getting money from the Gazette is on my list." Kara grimaced.

I handed her another paper. "And here's the list of Kicker parents you are to get to volunteer to be bus and hotel chaperons. We also have football game concession stands to man."

"Another of my favorite things, twisting people's arms to volunteer."

I sent her a commiserating look. "Comes with the territory." I waved my handful of pages with similar duties.

"I know." She sighed. "I'm happy to be doing all this because of what it means for the girls. But did they need to preach to us all night long? I don't think either of us got a word in. I hate being treated as if I didn't have a thought in my pretty-little-head."

Laughing, I got out of the car, then leaned back in. "You know what they say about you blondes...."

"Go to bed," Kara called as she put the car in gear. I slammed the door shut, still chuckling.

Despite making light of being treated so high-handedly by other officer mothers, it must have bothered me more than I realized. I didn't sleep well and had weird dreams.

In one, Kuddles yelled at me that Zoe stole all the chocolate bars the Kickers were to sell as a fundraiser. I screamed at her to leave my child alone, Zoe would never do something horrible like that. Then I wiggled my nose and turned Zoe back into a fourth grader, found the chocolate under her bed, and ate all the evidence myself before the Hansel and Gretel witch showed up.

When the alarm went off, I lay a moment as the silly dream dissolved into nothingness, replaced by thoughts of all I had to do that day. I flipped on the TV while I stretched before my run. One of my favorite Dallas reporters, Rex J. Fowler, was interviewing a young swimmer who had a chance to be on the US Olympic team. Her upturned nose and wide grin reminded me of Emily. It also reminded me that I needed to pick up chlorine. I probably looked forward to the lovely, lazy days of summer with kids hanging out at our pool as much as Zoe and Christopher did. Before I left the house, I added pool supplies to my long shopping list.

As the last month of school started, Zoe walked around with a bounce in her step that I'd never seen before. At first, I'd wondered if the three senior officers would accept the younger ones, but soon all six of the girls seemed thick as traffic on Woodall Rodgers at rush hour. I didn't immediately warm up to The Greats, but I had to give their moms credit; the girls had impeccable manners.

My son had a different slant on things. He and Zoe were scheduled for pictures for the newspaper one Friday near the end of the semester, he as a graduating senior next year and Honor Guard co-captain, and she as one of the new Kicker officers. They both wore their uniforms to school. The school's mascot was a huge cowboy, Giant Joe.

The dance team's field uniform consisted of white cowboy boots and hat worn with an emerald green mini-dress sporting a white, fringed, and sequined V-shaped overlay bearing the school logo. The girls wore matching, fringed, white gauntlets on their arms. A wide, white, leather belt circled the waist. Officers' hats were covered in white sequins.

The Honor Guard also dressed Texas style in starched Wrangler jeans and emerald green pearl-snap Western shirts, both cleaned and pressed crisply for free every week by one of the Duran's dry cleaners. Big silver buckles, cowboy boots, and black Stetson hats completed the boys' look.

When the kids got home from school, Zoe skipped off to her room. Christopher rooted around the fridge for a snack. He had frown marks marring his handsome face. Odd. He tended to be relaxed and good-humored. Nearly the polar opposite of his intense sister.

"How did things go today?" I asked from where I stood at the sink peeling sweet potatoes for dinner.

Christopher stood up, holding a baked chicken leg. "Fine, I guess."

I stopped working and narrowed my eyes at him. "You guess?"

He took a bite of chicken and chewed a moment, dropping a small bit on the floor for Andy who was nosing his leg.

"What's bugging you?" My mom radar pinged. "Is it something with Zoe?"

"Not exactly," he answered, his eyes on the chicken.

"Okay, mister. Quit being evasive. What is it?"

He moved a kitchen chair sideways and plopped down. At seventeen, Christopher was already a couple inches taller than his dad but slim and wiry. His long legs sprawled out in front of him, cowboy boots resting on the polished tile. "It's probably nothing, but you know all those Great officers have jock boyfriends."

"And?" I asked when he paused.

"It's probably nothing, but I just don't want Zo feeling pressured into thinking she has to have a boyfriend or date an athlete. She's only fifteen."

"She's level-headed," I said, but inside I wasn't feeling it.

Feeling pressured into having a boyfriend or dating was just like something Zoe would do.

Michael and I had discussed not wanting either of our kids to date in high school but rather to cultivate friendships and do things in groups. However, Michael had seen too much with his job to think forbidding a teenager to do something was the wisest way to discourage it. The last thing we wanted was the kids going behind our backs.

"Why are you worried about this?" I asked, hoping my voice sounded casual. "Did something happen?"

This time, Christopher's eyes definitely shifted away from mine. "It's probably nothing. I mean…it's normal for the senior officers to hang out with their boyfriends at lunch, but Zoe's joined them. It's mostly football players, basketball players, and The Great cheerleaders and dance officers. Not her usual group."

It seemed strange to hear him being negative about other kids, because one of the wonderful things about Christopher was that even though he played soccer, he got along with everyone. He never criticized people.

"Do Emily and Paige sit there, too?"

"I don't know if Paige has the same lunch period or not, but Emily does, and I've never seen her sitting with them."

He finished his chicken and obviously had gotten this concern off his chest, because he rinsed his hands and went to his room to change. A short time later, I heard him shooting hoops in the driveway.

I didn't get over our discussion so easily. My thoughts flashed as quickly as the peeler in my hand.

To think I'd only worried about her making officer. I'd never considered what might come along with the position. Had something happened between Zoe and Emily? They'd always eaten lunch together. They had been friends for years. I wondered if they'd had a fight and Zoe hadn't told me. It didn't seem likely. She seemed too happy. Maybe Emily was upset with Zoe, and my daughter was clueless. I didn't see a way I could find out or help.

School gets so busy the last few weeks that I hadn't seen Kara as much as normal. Usually, we talked over every little thing going on with the girls. But this didn't seem like something I could ask her, especially if Kara didn't know something was wrong. I didn't want to upset her for no good reason. I decided to ask Tracy when I took Zoe to her ballet class.

Instead of just dropping her off and running errands, I

followed Zoe inside the building. She walked past a dance room where Rochelle, Tracy's business partner, was teaching a class of very young girls. They were so cute, chubby-legged mini ballerinas. Zoe turned into the largest room. Mirrors ran the length of the high-ceilinged space reflecting the girls in black leotards and pink tights, their hair pulled up into buns.

I followed and stopped near Tracy who stood by the door greeting each dancer by name.

"Do you have a second?"

Tracy gave me a surprised look and glanced at the large clock on the wall. Class started in five minutes. Girls were filing into the room, putting down their dance bags, and chatting while they changed into pointe shoes.

"Sure. What's up?" she asked, moving off to the side away from students and moms.

A row of folding chairs sat under the window for those parents who chose to stay and watch the class. I dropped my bag on one and angled my back to the room, giving us a little privacy.

"It may be nothing, but have Emily and Zoe seemed any different since they became officers?" I asked in a low voice.

Tracy's large eyes searched the room, landing briefly on Emily who was already stretching at the barre. Zoe sat in a group of girls talking as they laced up their shoes.

"What do you mean?" she asked.

"You know how close they've always been, but now that they are officers…" my voice trailed off. I wasn't sure what to say. "I've wondered if their friendship is strained."

"Do they get along with the other officers?" Tracy asked, perched gracefully like a bird on one leg, the other foot resting against her thigh.

She'd always had a tiny, dancer's build, like Zoe. Years of dance training left Tracy with perfect posture that bordered on regal. If it weren't for the wild-colored hair and row of tiny diamond studs running around the shell of her left ear, I'd often thought she could pass for a princess. She loved to dress outlandishly, probably to offset her girly passion for ballet.

"They get along with the older officers for official Kicker business," I answered, bringing my mind back to her question, "but I'm not as sure about Emily outside of school stuff. Zoe seems to have clicked with them more than Emily has."

"Ah…The Greats," Tracy said. She flicked a quick look to where Isabella and Madison talked to Zoe. The third Great, Layla, took tap, not ballet or jazz which were Zoe and Emily's favorites.

"Are you worried this could be a problem between Zoe and Emily?" Tracy asked.

"I'd hate to think of anything coming between them.

Zo hasn't said anything, and I can't very well ask Kara if Zoe's cut her daughter out for new, cooler friends."

Tracy pushed a strand of fuchsia-tipped hair behind her ear. "I guess Kara might not feel like asking you about it either, huh? I see your problem."

That was one of the best things about Tracy. She got me. She always had.

Giving my arm a quick squeeze, she said, "I'll keep an eye on things and let you know what I think."

"Thanks." I grabbed my purse.

Tracy gave me a commiserating smile, turned and clapped her hands. "Ladies. Find your places, please."

As I left, I noticed Emily picked a spot across the room from Zoe.

All in all, I thought the end of school and the beginning of summer might be a very good thing.

Perhaps things would get back to the way they used to be.

Chapter Eight

Nervous Nellie

Present

"They finally let me in to see you."

At her voice, I turn my head. Kara edges into the room, a ridiculously large balloon bouquet in her hand. Orange and yellow Mylar globes bounce on the end of long ribbons. My favorite colors. Other balloons read, "Get Well Soon" and "We Miss You."

She walks in on tiptoes, as if footsteps might shatter me. "They wouldn't let me bring flowers into the ICU. Too many bacteria. Jeesh! And I shouldn't really be here at all, since I'm not family. So, I said I'm your sister. I think the nurse at the desk got tired of seeing m—" she breaks off, then laughs shakily. "I'm rambling."

Kara busies herself tying the balloons to a cabinet

handle. They float over the chair where Michael slept. At least, I think he slept there.

I'm not sure of anything. I figured out that I've been hallucinating. Not a great thing to realize but better than having a mind that isn't working at all. Everything seems so real when I'm imagining it.

Kara spends a ton of time getting the balloons floating just right. Finally, she turns around but doesn't look at me. It dawns on me that I must be a mess of bruises. Feels like it, anyway. My ribs hurt from the seatbelt and my face and arms are raw from the airbag.

"It's good to see you," Kara says, coming over to the bed. She still isn't looking at me though. She stares over my head. That monitor is so compelling.

"I'm glad to see you, too." My throat is dry. My voice scratchy. I take a sip of water. "But you sure seem to be a nervous Nellie."

"Oh, honey. I've been so scared. Not just me. The whole NEST is praying. The whole church, too." She giggles nervously again. "Heck, the whole town. Probably the whole state."

I reach out and put my hand on hers. "Thank you. Thank everyone for me, please."

Now, her eyes meet mine and she bursts out crying.

"Oh, Sheena. What a mess. I was so scared. Everyone was. Things are so bad already. I didn't want to lose you. I still need you. You're too young to die." She takes a gulp of air. "You're a miracle. An actual miracle."

Chapter Nine

New Friends, New Worries

Two Months Earlier

I didn't share Christopher's concerns with Michael or Zoe, but I kept an eye on her and listened carefully to what she and Emily talked about on the way to and from school.

I'd shared driving duties with Kara for years. She and I had quickly learned the value of carpool gossip, finding out what went on during the kids' days when they discussed it on the way home, or listening to their plans as we drove them to school. They were so used to us being in the car – the invisible chauffeur – that they let their guards down and discussed things they might not ordinarily have talked about in front of their moms. Who was going out with whom. What kid got nailed with pot in his locker. Why they were certain the mystery meat served in the cafeteria was roadkill.

Useful information.

It might have been my imagination, but things seemed more strained between them than normal. Their discussions continued to revolve around dance, not just High Kickers but ballet and jazz classes at Tracy's studio. They also talked over ideas for choreographing the drill team's field routines, which was what the Kickers worked on over the summer.

Graitney's school district was too small too to hire a professional choreographer as some large districts did. The officers were picked from those Kickers who had lots of years of dance experience and could help Miss Williams come up with the many routines they needed throughout the year. It was part of the fun of being an officer.

The girls also discussed which classes they would take the following year and the normal chit-chat about music and movies. But I noticed that Zoe mentioned the names Layla, Isabella, and Madison often. What The Greats thought of this song or that show. The cute new Miu Mui bag Layla had. The way Madison cut her hair. Emily listened politely but didn't add much.

Different guys' names cropped up in their conversation now. I listened carefully, but thankfully, I didn't hear any one boy mentioned more than any other.

Several times, I reminded myself not to get worked into a snit. It was normal for girls their age to be interested in guys. We were just fortunate the two of them haven't been boy-crazy for years.

School ended and I relaxed. I naively assumed this summer would be like all the others: Zoe, Christopher, and their church friends hanging out at our pool, having movie nights, or sleepovers at each other's houses. All under the supervision of parents I'd known since the kids were in kindergarten.

However, from the very first weekend, things were different.

Zoe found me in the laundry room where I stood sorting items the kids had outgrown into piles to be donated to the church's community outreach store. Anne perched on the edge of the countertop waiting for me to get distracted so she could curl up on the freshly laundered clothes. She bathed herself, getting her fluffy tail clean. Her long white fur shone.

"Mom, Madison is having some friends spend the night tonight to celebrate school being out. May I go?" Eager anticipation lit Zoe's face. She petted Anne and was rewarded with a thanks-for-messing-up-my-bath look. The cat lifted a dainty paw to her tongue, licked, and started bathing a silver-tipped ear.

I got that Zoe wanted to fit in with the other officers, but I didn't really know anything about their families other than The Blondes were a tight-knit group in a totally different socio-economic position than us. Rumors about the party and underage drinking last year raced through my mind, but that was unfair. It had involved Layla's older brother and his friends. I couldn't blame the sins of one sibling on another. Besides, The Blondes went to a church in town. Who was I to judge?

Stalling for time, I dumped a basket of clothes from the dryer onto the countertop. Anne moved forward and I shooed her back. "Just girls, right?"

The world may have changed from when I grew up, but Graitney was small enough that I didn't expect any parent had coed sleepovers.

Zoe rolled her eyes. "Duh."

Normally, we don't allow that expression, but I let it slide. It wasn't a hill I was ready to die on.

Picking up one of Zoe's childhood nighties with the Frozen princesses on it, my fingers rubbed the silky material.

"Is Emily invited?" I asked, remembering years ago when the girls had begged so hard that Kara and I had relented and bought them the matching nightgowns. Then we took their pictures in them.

They'd been so little and cute. We called Zoe and Emily "Night and Day" because of their opposite coloring. Zoe had refused to get rid of that nighty until it fit like a t-shirt.

"She's doing something with her grandparents," Zoe answered a little too quickly.

I folded the nightgown and reluctantly set it on the donate pile. "And Madison's parents will be there?"

She reached out and gave her old nighty an absentminded stroke, hesitating a fraction of a second before saying, "Of course."

Turning, I gave Zoe my full attention. "I'll just call Aimée and make sure."

Her entire frame collapsed. "Mo-o-om! You'll embarrass me. I'm not a third-grader."

I hesitated, knowing how important it was to Zoe to feel grown-up and included, but we'd always sheltered her. Heck, her dad threatened to run a background check on the poor boy who'd taken her to prom last spring, even though they'd gone in a group of ten kids, and I'd chaperoned the dance. Not that he would have, as it's against the rules.

"Okay, sweetie." She shouted with delight before I finished. "I guess you can go."

She skipped out of the room, and I turned back to my sorting, trying to reassure myself that I'd made the right decision. Anne leapt happily onto the warm pile of clothes, turned herself into a donut, and settled down, purring loudly.

What harm can a bunch of girls get up to while the parents are home?

A few hours later, I watched Zoe walk out the door with her overnight bag. She opened the door of Layla's BMW metallic-red convertible and slid inside. It slammed shut. She hadn't waved good-bye. A sour feeling washed over me, which I chalked up to normal mom-nerves.

As it was a Thursday night, I headed to Bible study. The NEST (Nurturing Each Sister with Truth) was the group of friends closest to me besides Kara and Tracy, both of whom were Chicks themselves.

Ever since Zoe made officer, I'd thought about asking the Chicks to pray for me to have wisdom about how to handle this new phase of her life. But that seemed silly. She was just a normal girl growing up. A couple of our members had some serious needs: marriage troubles, parents with dementia, a sister with cancer. My vague worries seemed so trivial.

We met at Gabby Guthrie's house. She greeted me at the door, the scent of fresh peanut butter cookies wafting out onto the warm night air. Almost as tall as me, she had beautiful prematurely white hair which she wore long. As she was a serious athlete, it was almost always up in a high ponytail. Her movements were quick, energetic and her countenance, as always, radiated joy.

"Hi, Sheena. Why the glum look?"

I hitched on a smile. "Sorry, Gabby. Zoe's off to a sleepover with her new Kicker friends. I'm a little concerned."

She held the door open. "Then you are at the right place. No worries allowed. Remember this week's homework was to cast all our cares on Jesus? We'll talk about how we each did with that."

Gabby lived in a large farmhouse, which the town now encompassed. Her furnishings tended toward comfy, just like the hostess herself. None of her furniture cost much, but she had a magic touch with paint and decorating. The whitewashed style with neutral colors made her house relaxing and inviting, fitting because she loved to entertain and surrounded herself with people. I'd never seen Gabby upset or discouraged. No matter what happened in life, she met it with a sincere "Praise the Lord," even last year during her mom's health battles and eventual death. People were drawn to her like kids to video games.

I strolled into the living room where a handful of other ladies already gathered. In the dining room, some were grabbing cookies and glasses of iced tea before finding seats. Ida, the wife of one of the town's most prominent business men, stood by the refreshment table.

"Congratulations, Sheena! I heard about Zoe making Kicker officer." She shot me a conspiratorial grin.

Her twin daughters, Lily and Olivia, were two years behind Zoe in school and took dance at Tracy's studio. The twins took after their father in looks, tall and willowy.

Rather short, Ida struggled constantly with her weight. To compensate, she dressed impeccably, kept a perfect tan, and had teeth bleached paper-white.

"*L&O* are already working on routines for next year's Kicker tryouts."

"Good for them." I grabbed an iced tea.

"My good friend, Kuddles, says they will be the first identical twins on the High Kicker drill team. Won't that be cute?"

I felt rather sorry for Ida. She wanted so badly to be part of The Blondes, even going so far as to bleach her dark brown hair an unflattering orange shade. She was wealthy enough to be in the clique, but her husband leased agricultural equipment to farmers. Not a glamorous occupation in the nouveau riche world of The Blondes who'd supplanted Graitney's old social strata, knocking her and others off their former perch when the town first started to grow.

I agreed, the twins were cute no matter what they were doing and she wandered off. Tracy came over. I hadn't seen her since I'd asked her to keep an eye on the girls. She smiled at me, and I relaxed. She was as comfortable as old slippers. We knew everything about each other, including what we were like before we were living as we should. I could talk to her about anything.

"How are Emily and Zoe doing?" she asked, grabbing

a cookie.

"They seem a little cooler than normal. What have you noticed?"

She took a bite and wiped crumbs off her lips before answering. "The same thing. Normally, I get on to them because they talk all through class. Now, Zoe and Madison are thick as thieves. Isabella hangs around Madison, like always, and Layla joins them after class. I get the feeling Em's being left out."

I frowned. "I don't like to hear that."

"How do you think The Greats are treating Zoe?" she asked, taking another bite.

"Maybe a little too good."

She cocked her head, cookie forgotten. "What do you mean?"

"Oh, I don't know. I want Zoe to be included, and she's incredibly happy, but I'm worried they'll be a bad influence on her. I mean they're a couple of years older."

"Afraid she'll follow in her mother's footsteps?" she asked, eyes teasing, before popping the rest of the cookie into her mouth.

I shushed her and looked around to see if anyone could overhear us. It wasn't like I was some perfect person or anything, but that old college life of hard drinking and poor choices was way behind me *and* Tracy. I desperately wanted it to stay there.

"Yeah," I whispered. "That's exactly what I'm worried about, not that I actually know anything about those girls. That's the problem. That and I don't want her cutting out old friends, especially a great girl like Emily." I chugged some tea.

"I get that." Tracy snatched another cookie.

I envied the way she could eat and stay thin as a straw. Probably all the exercise she got teaching dance. Fortunately, being tall, I'd never had a weight issue, but now that I was in my forties, I had to pay more attention to working out and not mindlessly eating.

Refilling my glass, I headed to the living room and sat down next to Dolores. She turned her long face toward me. Her downturned eyes tended to look sorrowful.

"Congratulations on Zoe making officer," Dolores said, sounding strained. "I hope it goes good for her."

Belatedly, I remembered her daughter, Jordan, a junior, had tried out, too.

"Thank you." I liked Dolores and sincerely wanted to make her feel better. "There were so many great candidates. It had to have been hard for the judges to choose."

It felt inadequate. Dolores gave me a sad little smile, as if seeing through but appreciating my effort. Thankfully, Gabby put on a worship song and the talk around the room ended as we rose to our feet to sing.

Kara, Mati, Tracy, and Cecilia scooted into the room, joining those already gathered. There was space next to me on the couch, but Kara took a seat across the room. Was she upset with me because Zoe was snubbing Emily?

Wonderful. One more thing to worry about.

"Let's start by saying our memory verse, James 1:2-4, to the woman sitting next to you," Gabby said after we finished singing and she prayed.

Cecilia turned to me and whipped out, "My brethren, count it all joy when you fall into various trials, knowing that the testing of your faith produces patience. But let patience have its perfect work, that you may be perfect and complete, lacking nothing."

She looked at me expectantly.

I stumbled through the verse, with a lot of glancing at my index card. Scripture memory was a spiritual discipline I meant to get better at but somehow didn't make time for. Gabby's voice rang in my mind, "When it comes to a battle with the enemy, I want my Sword of the Spirit to be three feet long and made of steel, not a plastic cocktail skewer."

Once again, I vowed to myself to do better.

"Perfect. Complete. Lacking nothing." Gabby looked around the room. "Isn't that the type of Christian we all would like to be?"

Everyone nodded.

"How do we become that way?" she asked.

Dolores groaned. "Through trials?"

"What does the Scripture say?" Gabby asked, waited a beat, then answered herself. "Through our *patience* in trials. We are not joyful *for* the trial itself but for the work God can do in our lives if we stay in faith and trust him no matter what."

She paused and I couldn't have been the only one of us thinking of how unshakable Gabby's faith had been through the hardship of losing a beloved parent.

"Do you see why we were to practice 1 Peter 5:7 this week? 'Casting all your care upon him, because he cares for you.' It would be hard to do one without the other. Hard to go through trials if Jesus wasn't shouldering the burden. Tell me how that went this week."

Two hours later, I felt completely at peace. The NEST was such a vital part of my week. Church and personal prayer time were important, but God had a way of bringing home lessons to me through the struggles and triumphs of my sisters in Christ. It helped to know I wasn't the only one struggling in certain areas. It's easy to have all the churchy answers. It's another to live out our faith.

Kara was deep in conversation with Mati and Gabby after the meeting, so Dolores and I walked to our cars together.

"I hope the girls aren't getting up to anything tonight," Dolores said.

She wrestled with so many things, always worrying, even though from the outside her life looked completely blessed.

I raised my eyebrows, realizing that her daughter, Jordan, must be spending the night at Madison's, too. How many girls were invited? The whole team or just select ones?

"Up to anything?" I repeated.

She gave an airy laugh, "Oh, you know how the Altermans are. The house is the size of a mall. The girls could be entertaining the football team at one end and the parents on the other side would never know. That's why the Kickers love hanging out there."

"They aren't known for exactly enforcing the rules, either, are they?" Cecilia said.

I hadn't heard her and Ida walk up behind us. Tiny, prim and proper, Cecilia was a stickler about everything, but since this might involve Zoe, she had my full attention.

"What do you mean?" I asked.

"The Altermans' oldest boy was in the same year as my Charles. Well it goes without saying, he was friends with Logan Malik and..." she let her voice fade away. "Let's just put it this way, it's a good thing they know bigshot lawyers and have the money to foot the bills."

"Oh, Cecilia," Ida said sharply. "Let's don't be spreading malicious gossip. My good friend Kuddles sings

Aimée's praises. Just because her boy Logan ran into a bit of trouble doesn't taint them all. I trust Aimée with my own darling *L&O*. And that's saying a lot."

We parted and got into our own vehicles, but the happy feeling I'd left Gabby's house with a couple of minutes before had dissipated more quickly than the May heat from my car with the AC cranked. I wanted to rush over and yank Zoe away from the slumber party.

I said out loud, "Okay, Sheena. Stop it! You are letting your thoughts run away with you. Don't do that. What did you just spend two hours discussing?"

Instead of letting myself go to the panic place, I spent the drive home praying and asking God to protect Zoe. Before getting into bed, I shot her a text: "Praying you and your friends are having fun."

Pretty good.

That should be a subtle reminder of who she is but also that I want her to enjoy her new status.

I didn't hear back.

Chapter Ten

Still No Answers

Present

Kara leans over and gives me an awkward hug and a
kiss on the forehead. "I promised the nurse three minutes,
tops. Just rest and get better. Everyone is praying and
pulling for you. No matter what."

She gives me one last smile, her eyes tear-bright, then
rounds the corner of the door and is gone.

No matter what? Am I not out of danger yet? Could I
relapse? I still can't remember the accident. I don't even
know where I was going. I try to put together the things
I've heard my family and the doctors say. Strings of words.

My mind works slowly. Stubborn. An engine refusing
to turn over and start.

"How are you feeling?" A nurse I've seen before

wakes me from a doze. "You had a pretty nasty case of acute sinusitis, a sinus infection, when you came in, besides all the trauma from the accident."

Her soft blue eyes are kind as she bustled around taking my vital signs. I'd grown used to this every-four-hour routine.

A flash of memory, I'd been sick before the accident. Really sick.

Now, every time I cough, my ribs hurt. Probably bruised by the seatbelt. My face is tender. Airbag?

I glance around the room expecting to see someone, but there's no one besides the nurse.

She reads my look. "You've had lots of friends come by, Mrs. McKenzie, but doctor's orders say family only until you're stronger."

Family only. I smile to myself. She hasn't come up against sneaky people like my friends Tracy and Kara. They found a way.

Time stretches and shrinks, jerks along strangely. I think I've just been talking to her, but the nurse is gone. Michael sits in the chair, elbows propped on his knees, watching me.

"Hi," he says when I open my eyes.

He must have gone home and done that washing

thing under running water because he's freshly shaved,
but I don't think he's slept. I've never seen him with purple
smudges under his eyes before.

"Hi." I try to sit up, but I'm attached to too many
things. Despite the tape, the IV pinches my skin where the
needle goes in. One little pain out of so many.

Michael jumps up and pushes a button on the side of
the bed. Like magic I'm suddenly sitting.

"Better?"

"Thanks." I wait while he sits down.

Not remembering details about the accident stresses
me. I can't think of how to ask him what I want to know
without blurting it out. Subtlety has left me. "I want to
know about the accident. Where was I going? What was I
doing? What happened?"

Michael's eyes study his clasped hands. An emotion
flashes across his features too quickly for me to read.
Mainly he looks resigned as he studies his knuckles.

Why will no one look at me? It makes me feel
ashamed and I don't know why.

There must be adult details, things about car repairs
and money and insurance, that I should ask about, but
they're vague concepts. Trying to grasp one is like
clutching smoke. If I'm this uneasy with no memory,

Michael must be under incredible stress.

Still, I've got to know something. "Tell me, Michael. What happened? I can't remember anything."

His grey-green gaze, so like Zoe's, slowly rises to meet mine. "Now isn't the time to talk about this, Sheena. You need to concentrate on getting well."

"Michael, please. I need answers."

His face looks bleak, his eyes immeasurably sad. "Trust me, She-Girl. You don't."

Chapter Eleven

Getting Anxious

Two months earlier

Michael came in from work and asked about the kids.

"Christopher's working. Zoe's sleeping," I said from the kitchen table where I was scrolling through Pinterest on my MacBook looking for something new to do with chicken breasts. "I hope this isn't going to become a habit this summer."

Layla had dropped Zoe off after lunch and she'd napped all afternoon. Seems her first sleepover with The Greats had worn her out.

"Let her relax," Michael answered, loosening his tie and unbuttoning the top button of his shirt. "School just ended. Her grades were great, and she worked hard to make officer. She deserves a bit of down time."

"Too bad she can't have a summer job like her brother.

Work builds responsibility."

"Yeah, like being a High Kicker officer isn't hard work." He grinned wryly and shook his head.

I went to the fridge and poured him a glass of iced tea. "True. Her summer will revolve around official Kicker activities. A job isn't practical."

Michael took the icy glass. "This summer being an officer *is* her job, and it will build responsibility."

He was right, of course. Why would I wish those carefree summer days away for my kids? Adult life comes too fast as it is, and I'm the one that wanted to keep her from rushing to grow up.

We talked about our day and some of the things going on around town as he helped me finish making dinner. Andy twined himself underfoot, hoping for people food. Michael kept sneaking him pieces of chicken and cheese. We woke Zoe and made her join us when supper was ready. I asked her what the girls had done at the sleepover.

"Oh, you know." Her eyes were on the fork as she pushed capers around on her plate. "Normal stuff."

Both Michael and I paused and looked at her, waiting for her to say more.

"Like?" I asked.

"Watched movies. Listened to music. Talked. Ate junk food. That kind of thing."

I opened my mouth again, but Michael shot me a look.

Nothing bad had happened. We knew because he had patrol cars cruise the area just to be sure there wasn't a raucous party going on.

Of course, like Cecilia said, the place was so large who knows what was going on inside just because it didn't spill over into the street. I decided to go with Ida's advice and trust these new moms. Just because I didn't know them, didn't make them unfit parents.

As the weeks went by, I grew used to The Greats popping in and out as regularly as Zoe's church friends used to do. Emily joined them whenever they were doing an official Kicker activity, but otherwise I didn't see her as often as in summers past. I continued to wonder if it was her doing or Zoe's and if Kara had noticed a change? But I still didn't know how to ask. Besides, I hoped I was imagining the whole thing and somehow it would work itself out.

Sleepovers at The Greats' houses continued, but as nothing bad happened, I finally relaxed on that score. Something else began to bother me.

Zoe seemed a lot more secretive than before. She spent more time alone in her bedroom than in the family room. If I walked in unannounced, she turned her iPad over or laid her phone down, so I couldn't see what she'd been doing. When I asked what was up, she told me she was just keeping up with friends on social media.

Probably normal teenager behavior. Still…

I mentioned it to Tracy, who said Zoe was a great kid, and I didn't need to fret. It wasn't as reassuring as I'd hoped. Even though she taught a lot of teenagers, she didn't have children of her own. It wasn't really the same. Kara would be the friend I'd normally talk to about things like this but being unsure of Emily and Zoe's relationship made me keep my concerns to myself.

That left Michael. I hated to bother him about my worries because he had so much going on at work. He worked unusually long hours, taking calls 24/7, and for a laidback man, he seemed distracted.

"There are just some extra things going on at work right now," he said when I brought it up one evening while I skimmed the pool and he checked the chlorine level.

"Anything I should know about?"

He held the little colored container up to see if things needed adjusting. "No. Just be glad we've got such great kids doing normal things. I feel bad for some of the parents out there."

Michael had quit bringing home specifics about his job a long time ago because he didn't want me to worry about him or what was going on in our town, especially if it involved kids. On that score, I was a total wimp. I couldn't even read books or watch movies about missing children. As to all the stuff teens in cities got up to? Forget it. I couldn't even think about those things.

But we weren't as isolated as we'd once been.

Being within driving distance of Dallas and Fort Worth, the small city of Graitney was booming. Transplanted Californians flocked here after a major company relocated its headquarters nearby. Their money went a lot further in Texas than it did in the Golden State. We'd gone from sleepy farming town to North Texas suburb in a few short years.

"We didn't used to have big city crime," Michael had grumbled shortly after becoming chief. "Rural problems no longer."

Not everyone from this small town in the buckle of the Bible Belt liked the influence of the new folks from the West Coast. The debate among our church friends over the newcomers had been heated.

"I'd never allow my children to be in our public schools," Cecilia insisted. "Too many bad influences."

We didn't have a Christian school, and quite a few of our friends homeschooled. However, Michael felt that as a public servant, he had an obligation to have his children attend public schools. For the most part, I agreed. It let our kids have opportunities like being on the soccer, dance, and spirit teams. But as the summer wore on, I began to wonder about that decision.

On the one hand, Zoe seemed more confident and sure

of herself with her new friends, but I was still unsettled by the fact that The Greats' parents weren't people I'd known and trusted for years. Even though the girls spent a lot of time together, the adults were a close-knit clique. I'd never be one of them. Wasn't sure I'd want to be.

Still, it bugged me. I wondered about the values they'd taught their daughters, even though I couldn't put my finger on anything they were doing wrong. What disturbed me the most was not only Zoe being more secretive, but she'd grown distant. We'd always had a close relationship and spent a lot of time together.

Being honest with myself, I realized I was jealous that I'd been supplanted.

I brought it up one night at the NEST and a couple of ladies with older kids assured me this was normal. All teenagers pulled away at some point. That didn't make me feel better. My job as a mother was to protect my children. How could I do that if I didn't know what was going on with her?

Since Christopher had come to me with his concerns before, I decided to pump him for information. He worked late as a waiter most nights, so both kids had gotten into the habit of sleeping in. Then he'd meet his buddies at the gym. In the afternoon, he'd have friends over to swim or do something else together before getting ready for work.

It took a few days to catch him alone. I found him

playing on his Xbox. I knocked on his bedroom door. He gave me a glance and a nod, mumbling for me to wait a second.

I entered his room and perched on the end of his bed, trying not to get too close, because I'd felt crummy for a couple days. Now it was worse. I was coming down with a summer cold.

Curled up next to him, Andy opened sleepy eyes and gave a huge yawn. I rubbed the cat's head. He sent me a disgruntled look for interrupting his nap. He made a show of moving to the other side of the bed, winding himself up in a circle, and lying back down.

I tried to watch Christopher play. My eyes couldn't track as fast as the soldiers on the screen were shooting. Incredible. It showed the difference between the kids' teenaged lives and my own. I was busy, but they were busier, involved in so many things and constantly on the go, either in person or plugged in digitally. When had everything, even games, sped up so much?

After a few minutes, he stopped playing and laid down the controller. "What's up, Mom?"

Trying to sound casual, not panicked, I said, "I just miss seeing as much of you and your sister this summer as usual. Your lives are so hectic."

He scooted back against his headboard as if settling in to talk. A good sign.

"Yeah, sorry. Next summer will be even worse, you know. I've decided to go to Fish Camp a few weeks before college starts."

At the thought of not having Christopher around, I swallowed around a soccer ball-sized lump in my throat. He'd decided to attend Texas A&M while in middle school. The kind of kid who had his whole life planned out since he was twelve.

"Do you have a pause button I can push?" My jocular tone sounded forced.

He wasn't fooled. Now, he looked uncomfortable.

I put a hand on his arm. "It's perfectly normal for kids to be in a hurry to leave the nest and for moms to want to keep them close. But that's kinda what I want to talk to you about. I'm worried about your sister. Have you noticed anything going on with Zoe?"

Christopher's gaze shifted away. "What do you mean?"

"Like maybe with the new girls she's hanging around with. The other officers."

"I really haven't seen her much lately." His eyes focused on a spot in the area rug where long ago a puppy had chewed a hole near his dresser.

I still missed that sweet dog. Irrationally, the thought made it feel like everyone was leaving me.

"That's what I mean. None of us have seen her very

much. That's not like the old Zoe."

He finally looked at me, worry stamped on his face. "I know."

I waited for him to go on.

"I've heard some things."

"Some things like?" Suddenly, I wasn't sure I wanted to hear what he had to say, but I had to.

"Nothing unusual for that group," he answered slowly.

My gaze bored into him. "What isn't unusual?"

He shrugged, clearly uneasy. "Well, the guys…their boyfriends hang around the girls all the time. Some of them are big partiers. You know, drinking and stuff."

The bottom of my stomach swooshed away.

"You didn't think this was information you should share with your dad and me?" My voice sounded sharper than I meant it to be.

Christopher looked hurt. "Don't be mad at me. Dad knows. Why do you think he has the guys patrol those neighborhoods? He can't do anything if it's in the privacy of someone's home."

"He can't do something about underage drinking?"

"I don't *know* that's going on. And Dad can't do anything, even if it is. They have to be caught first. Those older guys learned their lesson last year. Even kids have figured out to use designated drivers or just sleep over."

"Sleep over?" My pitch went up an octave. "Are you

saying the boys are drinking and sleeping over at the houses with the girls?"

Christopher shrugged. "No idea. They aren't the people I hang out with."

That was for sure. I'd never worried about him for a moment. Now, I felt sick thinking of what Zoe might have been exposed to. What she might have been up to. Was this what all the secrecy was about? What was she hiding from me? What was Michael hiding from me? Did he suspect this and not tell me?

Hot fury roiled inside me. I couldn't wait until Michael or Zoe got home. The first one through that door would feel my wrath spew over like a pot boiling over.

Chapter Twelve

A Perfect Idiot?

Present

Days. Minutes. Hours. Concepts I should know but that no longer seem to apply. I've no idea how long I've been in this bed. Or been awake this time.

When I talk, I lose simple words. Like squeezing a wet bar of soap, the harder I try the more the thought slips away.

Dr. Kraus strides in while doing his rounds.

"Mrs. McKenzie, your blood numbers are looking better. Thankfully, your blood pressure and oxygen level have stabilized, but I'm still hesitant to release you, as we aren't a hundred percent sure of what caused the initial idiopathic problem you presented with. You seem to have suffered a perfect storm of a number of factors."

What? I try to decipher his words. Thoughts themselves still ooze through my brain like Brie through a colander. By the time I work out the questions to ask, he's left the room. On to the next patient. This large city hospital keeps the staff hopping.

I go over what he said. My initial what kind of problem? Idiot problem. A perfect idiot? That can't be right. I'd been in a car accident. What things are they treating? A gash on my thigh. I lost so much blood I'd gotten several transfusions. Lots of bruising. I'd been knocked out or something which caused all the troubles with my stupid brain. What else? I can't remember.

I do have a perfect idiot problem. Me!

If only I could put together everything they've told me. I struggle to find memories. It's so frustrating. Like the critical piece of a puzzle missing after you've spent hours getting the other five hundred put together.

Those cardboard things are called puzzles, aren't they? Maybe this is all one giant puzzle. The kind you have when you're asleep.

I hope so.

Chapter Thirteen

All Hell Breaks Loose

The Day Before

As it turned out, Michael came through the door first. A detached part of my mind registered how drawn he looked, his eyes bleak, his normally upright bearing slumped with fatigue. I didn't care. The rage inside me had grown, horrible scenarios of what Zoe and her "friends" could have been up to festered in my imagination. All night parties. Binge drinking. Pot smoking. Zoe making out with guys we'd never met. Hard drugs. Worse?

"Why didn't you tell me what's been going on with Zoe?"

Surprised, he stopped, not even through the door yet.

"How do you know ab..." he started to ask, then stopped. "W*hat* do you know?"

"What do *you* know?" I shot back, my arms gripped

across my chest. I had to pull back for him to get into the house.

Michael closed the door and came inside, running a hand over his damp forehead, before wiping it on his pants. It was 101° outside. His bangs stood straight up in a way I'd normally find adorable. He went to the fridge and pulled out a Dr. Pepper. I drummed my fingers against my arm.

He took his time popping the top. The sound of pressure escaping hissed into the pregnant silence. Michael turned to me.

In the gentle voice he used when breaking the news of a fatality to a family, he said, "Let's go in the other room and sit down. We need to talk."

That tone instantly doused the furnace of fury burning in my belly, replacing it with icy dread. Maybe I really didn't want to know what he knew.

Shutting my eyes for a moment, I took a fortifying breath. The bug I'd been fighting grew worse by the hour. Grabbing a tissue, I blew my nose, and trailed behind him into the family room. Michael collapsed into his recliner. I sat opposite him, rigid on the edge of the couch.

We looked at each other for a long moment. He didn't seem to know where to begin.

Finally, he took a drink, set the can down on a coaster, and said, "Sheena, I just found out about Zoe being mixed up in the pornography thing this morning. I wouldn't have kept it from you."

My mind spun. Pornography? Were the girls looking at porn at those sleepovers?

"What are you talking about?" My hand curled around a throw pillow, and I pulled it against my chest like a shield.

Michael studied me curiously. "What were *you* talking about?"

The anger rushed back. "I'm talking about what happens at The Greats' houses during those sleepovers. Christopher told me that you've been aware this whole time that they have their boyfriends over. They may drink and do other things…I don't even want to think about what other things…."

Michael didn't say anything, just nodded ever so slightly.

"How could you let Zoe go to those houses?" The furious sound of my voice echoed around the room, bouncing off the hard wood floors, ricocheting off the cathedral ceiling.

"First off, Sheena, you were as aware of what went on with some of that group last summer as I was," he said with infuriating calm.

He'd had lots of practice soothing upset people. In his job as Chief of Police, he often dealt with angry citizens or problems within the seventy-five-person department. He also worked at the command level with personnel from other law enforcement agencies. Strong personalities all used to getting their own way.

Michael was great at staying in control when people around him lost their cool. It was one of the things I liked best about him. Yet for some unfathomable reason, I wanted him to be as upset as I was. He was Zoe's parent, too.

He went on, "There's no evidence of illegal behavior, but I thought you understood that's why I've increased patrols in those areas."

I slumped a little. I did know that.

"What's this about porn?" I asked in a more modified tone, fiddling with a tassel on the pillow. "What did you find out this morning?"

He took another gulp and swallowed. "Let me back up for a moment first."

I braced myself. It had to be bad if Michael needed to give me background before telling me what was going on.

"About six months ago, I was notified by an FBI task force of a problem in our area and asked to assist in an investigation. An investigation into pornography."

"Our girls have been looking at pornography?"

It seemed inconceivable. Raising a young man in today's world, I knew we might come up against this problem with Christopher but Zoe?

"Our kids *are* the pornography." His face looked as if his heart was breaking. "A person or persons have been targeting teenagers in the DFW area."

I stared at him. His words made no sense. None. The sweet little girl I raised – the one who delighted in twirling circles in the grass, her arms outstretched, face to the sun; the child who rescued every homeless puppy and kitten she came across; the girl baptized at the tender age of six – would never be involved in something so sordid. Something so demeaning.

"What are you talking about?" I was furious again, my voice lashing. "Zoe would never do anything that…disgusting…that filthy."

His eyes closed briefly before looking at me. He seemed to have aged. Michael set the can down gently and leaned forward, forearms on his thighs.

"No, I don't think Zoe would do so if she knew where the pictures would ultimately end up."

"Pictures?"

I knew pornography involved pictures, but hearing the word in connection with my precious daughter made the whole conversation too ghastly and real.

"Zoe may have thought she was sending them to a boy she liked. That's what many of the girls think."

Looking at Michael, I didn't see him. Instead, the awful realization of what he was telling me filled my mind.

Images I couldn't stop. My slim, beautiful daughter with her dancer's body. Just the sort of nubile young woman a pervert would desire.

Clapping a hand over my mouth, I jumped up, tossed the pillow away, and sprinted to the powder room, barely making it. I threw up, then started to shake.

Michael came in behind me after I rinsed my face and waited to see if my gut would quit churning. He slid his hands around me and pulled me close while I stared down into the toilet and wept.

Please, God. Don't let this be happening, please!

Chapter Fourteen

A Parent's Worst Nightmare

It took a good thirty minutes and a mug of strong hot tea with lots of sweetener and cream for me to quit crying and shaking. Even then, I didn't feel strong enough to hear the rest of what Michael had to say. My stomach continued to heave. I hoped the tea would stay put.

"I don't understand," I said as we finally sat back down.

Now, I prayed neither of the kids would get home before we got through all this and I understood what was happening. As Zoe's parents, we needed time to work out how to respond.

"She took pictures of herself, and they ended up on a website, but she didn't know what she was doing?" I reiterated. "This makes no sense."

"We won't know exactly what Zoe was thinking until we talk to her. As I said, I was notified that our local kids were specifically being targeted. It goes on across the country, of course. Actually, it's a global issue. But this perp or group of them was focusing on our North Texas kids. The parents of a child in town contacted the Dallas office of the FBI's Violent Crimes Against Children Unit. We've been working with them ever since."

That's what had been keeping him so busy.

"How? How do these perverts get to our children? I thought this was a problem for the poor kids in third-world slums. Some of the charities we support work to fight human trafficking."

My mind refused to accept what it was hearing. There had to be a mistake. This kind of thing doesn't happen to American children. Not my American child.

"True, but, sadly, it is a problem here, too. There are people who target kids from bad home situations and runaways. But all young people, no matter what their background, are at risk. Our teens live online. Even younger children, too. These predators troll popular social media sites and find their victims. Then they blackmail them into sending photos or videos. Sometimes they trick the kids into thinking they are another teenager and get the same result."

"Zoe wouldn't fall for something like that." I hugged

the pillow against my still roiling stomach.

"These guys are incredibly good at their scams. They'll search for a young girl who loves to take selfies and videos."

My voice was leaden, "Like Zoe."

"Like Zoe. And message them. They say that they already have a nude picture of them and will send it to all their friends if they don't send more photos."

"If the girl hasn't posted any nude pictures, why would she fall for that?"

"Think about it for a moment." His haunted gaze held mine. "Where do the girls keep their laptops or iPads, their phones?"

"In their bedrooms." I pulled my legs up under me and squeezed the pillow tighter.

"Right. So, they assume they left the webcam on by accident, or that someone hacked it and caught them undressing. Other girls are simply naïve. In fun, or on a dare, they send a video of themselves flashing their breasts or maybe a nude photo to a friend. Even if they use Snapchat and assume it disappears in a couple of seconds, they're in trouble."

I said dully, "People can screenshot the image. There are tons of websites telling people how to recover Snapchat pictures off their devices, too. Kara wanted to do that once with a lost vacation photo."

"More likely, a skilled predator will simply get a young person to believe they already have a photo. Then once the child sends another one, bingo, he's got all the blackmail power he wants. He can get the kids to keep sending more and more disgusting images, sometimes it goes on for years."

The air felt heavy and oppressive as this horror sunk in. The sharp scent of sick clung to me. My mouth tasted nastily of too much sweetener, cream, and vomit. I tried to swallow with a throat scratched raw.

"It goes on for years?"

"Usually, the victims don't tell anyone."

"Not even their parents? Why not?"

"They're scared this secret will get out and the lewd things they are being asked to do will go viral. Often the men pick socially visible girls, like Zoe, who are on the dance team or cheerleaders. They're scared of what their friends will think. Almost nothing matters more to a teenager."

Didn't I know.

"The predators might find girls involved in church activities, or those whose parents have prominent positions."

"Like you," I said. The twisted brilliance sunk in. "They'd be scared of hurting or shaming their parents."

"Right. The kids think they are avoiding the public

embarrassment of being thought of as slutty by their friends and hurting or getting into trouble with their parents."

"How do the creeps know all this stuff about them?"

Michael didn't even have to answer.

I sighed. "All that information is available online. Everything is online. No matter how careful we think we're being, our kids live online."

Our eyes met, commiserating. "How bad is what..." I couldn't bring myself to ask. "What about Zoe's pictures?"

"Good news. Bad news," Michael said, without the slightest hint of his normal humor. "This is by far the worst thing I've ever dealt with professionally." His voice was harsh. "Having to know what someone did to my own daughter."

"The good news?" I asked, praying this is all a mistake and it was actually another girl who looked like Zoe. God forgive me for wishing that on anyone.

"The good news is we may have caught this early. Her pictures are tame compared to a lot of the filth out there. Generally, the longer they go, the worse they get."

His hands balled into fists. "Of course, all of it is sick."

"You had to look at pictures of your own daughter?"

Michael looked as ill as I felt. I could not imagine the horror he'd been going through.

"No." He shook his head. "Never. The FBI has trained investigators who scan the crime scene for anything that might give us a clue as to who the child might be, the rest of us see only the child's face to help us identify them." Every muscle in him looked tense, ready to snap someone's neck in two. He continued to clench his massive fists.

I would hate to be the pervert behind all this if my husband was there on the take-down.

He clamped his jaw so hard, I could see a muscle twitching. With a visible effort, Michael wrestled himself back into control. He took a deep breath and his voice resumed its calm tone. "We think she's just begun sending the pictures, and that she's not being blackmail—"

"Who's not being blackmailed?" Zoe asked from the doorway.

Neither of us had heard her come in.

Chapter Fifteen

Innocence Gone

Michael and my eyes met for a fleeting moment before turning to our daughter. She looked so innocent standing there, a teasing smile on her lips. Strands escaping from a high ponytail curled around her face. The dark color contrasted with her light skin making her eyes look even larger and more doll-like than usual.

She's only a child!

Zoe wore jean cutoffs and a sea-green tank top that matched her eyes. How had I never realized quite how filled out she'd become, or that those shorts, which used to be modest, now barely skimmed her bottom? She hadn't been interested in boys, and looked young for her age, so I'd never been unduly worried about how she dressed. Especially as it was so much more appropriate than a lot of her peers.

Now, I saw her through completely different eyes. When had she developed such blatant sex appeal? Would I ever be able to look at my daughter without seeing her through the eyes of a predator?

She must have read something on our faces.

"What's wrong?" Zoe slipped across the room and sat down beside me, closer than normal, as if she needed her mom to protect her.

If only I could.

If only I had!

Michael cleared his throat. "Kiddo, this is difficult, but during an investigation, we came across pictures you sent to Andrew Hobart. Would you mind telling us who he is?"

"What investigation?" she asked, her voice rising. She looked back and forth between the two of us. "Have you been snooping in my stuff? I can't believe you would do that!"

"No, this has to do with work," Michael said heavily.

"Work?" Again, a quick look at both of us. "What? Like police work?"

He nodded. "We are investigating local child pornography."

Zoe gave a relieved bark of laughter. "Drew would never have anything to do with pornography or children. Or anything so disgusting."

She scooted away from me on the couch, drawing her knees up defensively. I turned to see her better, my heart breaking. She was so clueless.

Like I'd been such a short time ago.

"Who is this man?" Michael's asked again, his tone brooking no argument.

"He's...he's not a man. I mean...I guess he is. Andrew...Drew is eighteen. He's a senior at Plano East High."

"Eighteen? A senior in high school?" Michael's eyebrows scrunched together and he shook his head sadly.

He leaned forward as far as possible, bridging the gap between chair and couch. He had to be aching to reach her. To hug her.

"Actually, he's not either of those. We suspect Andrew Hobart is one of the aliases used by an older man. He's been at this for years. We found an elaborate office set up under a fake name in a climate-controlled storage unit in Arlington. He had pictures of you on his computer."

"You're lying." Zoe leapt off the couch.

She'd never talked to her father like that before.

"Sweetie, just listen to what your da—" I started.

"No!" She stamped her foot. "I knew you wouldn't like it that I have a boyfriend, so I didn't tell you. But I never thought you'd go this far. Snooping into my private life and lying to me."

I jumped up and grabbed her arm as she started to dash from the room. "Wait, Sweetie, you actually know this Hobart boy?"

"Of course, I do," Zoe said, stopping short. Her eyes beseeched me. "We met a couple of months ago. He's a buddy of Madison's boyfriend, Justin."

Our daughter had a relationship, obviously a sexual one, with a man we knew nothing about. I was still praying this was all a huge mistake and any moment I'd wake up from this nightmare. "Come on. Sit back down. Tell us about it, please?"

Michael shifted in his chair, a mass of restrained energy, but he didn't say anything. Zoe sat back down on the edge of the seat, ready to bolt.

"Like I said," she went on, looking mulish, "we met at a party." She must have caught the look on my face. "Ohh, Mo-om, it was just some friends of Madison's that dropped by one night when we were all hanging out. No big deal. Her parents were there."

She shook her head and rolled her eyes as if she knew this was how we'd react. "The other girls all have boyfriends. I'm the only one who doesn't...didn't...anyway they were kind of..." she paused, perhaps searching for a word that wouldn't make us cringe, "kind of paired up, and that just left Drew and me. We were alone in the hot tub..."

I groaned and Zoe shook her head again.

"...no big deal. Any way we kinda hit it off. We took some goofy pictures of each other, which we posted on PartyPlace. Everyone uses it. See? Nothing to it. That's how we got together."

There's a lot more to it than that, if there are nude pictures involved I wanted to scream, but I bit my tongue.

"Do you see Andrew often?" Michael asked, surprising me by how gentle his voice sounded. I wanted to yell at her.

For the first time, she looked embarrassed not defiant. "No, not in person. Not since that night. We make plans, but things happen. I mean, we don't even live in the same town, and I've only got my learner's permit. He messaged me right away the next day. We mainly text and..."

Zoe must suddenly have remembered how the conversation started because her face flamed, and she squared her shoulders. "I'm an adult and can have adult relationships."

I wanted to point out that in no one's world except a teenaged mind would fifteen years old be considered an adult.

"Do the other girls do...this..." I couldn't bring myself to say it, "do this picture thing with their boyfriends?"

Zoe shrugged her shoulders and went from looking defiant to embarrassed. "I don't know. I mean, this isn't something we go around talking about."

I'd been ready to string each one of those Greats up by their sequined overlays. At least, it hadn't been them that led her down this unthinkable path.

"These are private things. Just between Drew and me. He thinks I'm the most beautiful girl he's ever seen. He loves to be able to see me when we aren't together..." her voice trailed away.

All three of us sat thinking of just what was being seen.

"It isn't Andrew who messaged you," Michael said, his voice gentle. "He's not who you've been sending pictures to."

"He is too! How dare you say it's some old perv person." She crossed her arms and glared at us.

"Because our task force raided the storage unit of a Chase Reynard a week ago and found pictures of over 120 minors on his computer. Boys and girls."

"Ew-w-w," Zoe said.

"Yours were on there too."

She collapsed back, shrinking into herself. "He must have hacked Drew's computer and—"

"He's definitely a hacker. He probably found Drew's name when you posted your pictures. Then it was easy for a person with his skills to find out all the information he needed to pretend he was a teenaged boy you'd met only once." Michael looked at her with compassion and sadness etched on his face.

"Do you and Drew talk on lots of sites, or do you have a private one just for the two of you?"

"Private," she admitted reluctantly. Arms and legs crossed tightly, she angled herself away from us. "Drew hasn't found a way to break up with his long-time girlfriend yet. He doesn't want to hurt her feelings. Besides, he plays football and two-a-days have started. He's super busy."

"It wasn't Drew," Michael repeated.

We sat in silence, waiting for his words to sink in.

Zoe shook her head. "No, I don't believe you. Drew and I love each other...we made plans...I'm going to Texas Tech, like him, when I graduate, so we can be together. We're going to get married after I get my degree."

The magnitude of the effort the sicko had gone to in snaring our innocent daughter had me incredulous. But then basically, Zoe had been raised with good standards. It would have taken the pressure of her new friends all having boyfriends and a seasoned con-artist to talk her into what she'd done. Michael tried to explain this to her.

"Sweetie, all those plans and intense conversations online were with a mature man who knows how to emotionally manipulate a young woman. He used the appeal, personality, and supposed affection of a real young man – Drew – to fuel his power over you these last few months. To get you to do what he wanted."

"Dad," the pleading in her eyes matched her tone, "Drew loves me. He's my boyfriend."

"Kiddo, the real Andrew Hobart would be very surprised to find out you'd been sending him nude pictures."

She deflated like a punctured balloon.

Michael explained more about what they found during the raid. He answered each of her questions. At some point, my mind became numb to everything but the horror of what had happened to our daughter.

Zoe bit her lip a moment, looking ready to cry. "You're sure, then? You are sure some other guy was...is looking at me?" Her hand flew to her mouth. "Oh, my gosh! Someone from your work has seen my pictures, too?"

"I'm so sorry. Peop –" Michael's voice cracked and he started again. "People at the FBI crime lab have to sift through the evidence. They attempt to find all the victims. Hopefully identify the perpetrator. We need to convict this guy because he'll keep on doing this with other kids until he's caught. And..."

He stopped short.

I shot him a look and so did Zoe. "And what, Dad?"

Michael took a deep breath and let it out before replying. "I know this is hard to hear, but many of these predators – these sextortionists – barter the lewd images they have for child pornography from other men. They trade pictures with one another."

"What, like baseball cards?" I couldn't stop myself from asking.

He nodded. We both starred at him, absorbing this. I didn't know if I could take any more. How could Zoe?

Her voice quavered. "You mean my *private* pictures are somewhere out on the Internet for everyone to see?"

Michael looked as if he'd rather have shot himself with his pistol than answer the way he had to. "Yes, kiddo. Probably so."

"Can't you or somebody? The FBI or someone take them down? Delete them?"

I knew the horrible answer. "Once something is online, it's out there forever."

Chapter Sixteen

Endless Night

What followed felt like the longest night of my life. Michael went back to work. It was what he did. I knew every cop-molecule of his being yearned to bring the man who'd ruined our child's life to justice.

After our confrontation, Zoe stalked off to her room and shut herself in. Her sobs came from behind the closed door. Finally, I couldn't take it anymore, so I went to her room and knocked.

"Sweetie, can I come in?"

"No! Go away. Leave me alone."

"I just want to see if you're okay," I pleaded.

"I'm not okay. I'll never be okay." Something crashed against the wall. "My life is over."

I tried the doorknob, but it wouldn't turn. "Let's just

talk for a moment. Things aren't as bad as they seem right now."

"Yes, they are," she screamed, "and you're lying if you say they aren't."

She had me there.

"You're right, sweetie," I said. "This sucks. I can't even imagine how you're feeling."

I could think of one thing that felt worse – being the mom who just discovered she'd been unaware of her own child's sexual exploitation.

"No. You can't imagine how I'm feeling. No one can. Now, everyone will think I'm a fallen woman. A slut. A…a."—she was searching for something even worse to call herself – "a whore." Zoe barked a harsh laugh full of loathing. "That's hilarious. A virgin whore. I wish I was dead."

My heart seized with a new fear. "Oh, sweetie, don't say that."

"Why? I thought this family was all about the truth." Another horrible, mirthless laugh. "Well, isn't the family of the Chief of Police, this good Christian family, going to love the truth about their slutty, naked daughter being splashed all over everyone's computers and laptops and phones."

Her words made my stomach spin like a washer on agitate. Thankfully, there was nothing left in it.

"You guys have always been ashamed of me because I'm not as smart or as popular as Christopher. Well, now the world knows you have every reason to be ashamed of me."

"Zo, how can you say that? You are every bit as smart as your brother. People like you. You guys are just different from each oth—"

"Shut up! Shut up! Go away!" Her fists pounded the door. "I'm done talking. Leave me alone."

Each word caused me physical pain. Her fists pounded my gut, not just the door. A crushing weight squeezed my chest, not helped by the nasty cold raging full-force now. My head pounded and felt like it would explode. I went to the bathroom and slugged some nighttime cold medicine. Not that I expected to sleep.

I didn't.

All night, images of facing family and friends after they found out about Zoe's pictures tormented me, followed by rushes of guilt for feeling that way.

I'd stand by my kids no matter what they did.

I tried praying, but the bedroom ceiling seemed to have a non-stick coating. The prayers slid right off like scrambled eggs from a skillet. My entire adult life, Jesus had been my closest relationship. I could turn to and trust him in every situation. Now, when I need him the most, he felt further away than the stars winking outside the window.

God, I asked you to protect her. How could you let this happen?

I lay there straining to hear if Zoe left her room, terrified she'd...*do what?* I couldn't even put words to my fears. Did we have pills in the house that would harm her? I didn't think so. We were healthy. None of us had prescription meds.

Like every cop, when Michael went out, he kept his service weapon on him. The others were in a gun safe. Rigorous about gun safety, he'd taught both kids a proper respect for weapons at an early age. Only he knew the combination to the gun safe. The backup key was in the safe deposit box.

Zoe couldn't drive legally yet. She only had her learner's permit. Of course, that wouldn't stop her if she was determined to run away or crash a car. Around midnight, I gathered up all the sets of car keys I could find and hid them in my underwear drawer.

My brain would not turn off. Even though I didn't want to, my eyes continually checked the clock. 2:00. 2:36. Would this night ever end? 3:14. 3:45. 4:01. The interminable night crept by. Anne finally got tired of my tossing and turning and went to find a more peaceful place to sleep.

Sometime after four, I must have dozed, because the

next thing I knew it was six o'clock and nearly sunrise. Early light lit the bedroom a dove grey. There was no way I'd go back to sleep. Michael wasn't in bed. Hadn't he come home?

I padded barefoot down the hall. Walking past Zoe's closed door, I paused a moment with my ear against it, hearing nothing. I headed downstairs to the kitchen and coffee maker. A soft snoring came from the living room. Michael lay stretched out in the recliner, fast asleep. The table light still burned beside him. A murder mystery lay open on his lap.

Tiptoeing over, I turned off the light. For a moment, I watched him sleep, wanting to brush a kiss into his thick black hair. I craved the feel of him, the comforting scent that was all his own, but I didn't want to wake him. He'd looked so exhausted lately and now this. There was no way he'd gotten any more sleep than I had.

As I turned to go, an arm snaked around my middle. Michael pulled me onto his lap and snuggled me to him. I nuzzled my nose against his temple, my favorite place to smell him, as well as the kids when they were little. Even though Michael had to spend a lot of time indoors, he always had an outdoor scent that reminded me of sunny days spent in tree-forts.

His arms holding me tight felt great. I needed comforting.

"How are you doing?" he asked.

"Not good. You?"

A sigh billowed through his large chest. "Same."

I didn't kiss him, since I felt so awful. We sat quietly, just holding each other. What could we say, really? After a few precious minutes, we got up and headed to the kitchen. He made coffee while I pulled out oatmeal and fruit.

"Any luck last night?" I asked.

He looked at me from where he stood scooping an extra spoonful of grounds into the machine.

"No. I've been over everything we know so far. I just hoped something else would pop. Maybe help identify some other kids. See if any others are local. The rest is way beyond my expertise. The only reason we even found this guy is he made a mistake. He'd been using proxy servers that routed his stuff through South America and Eastern Europe."

Michael started the coffee, then sat down at the table. "Our lucky break came when one of the kids he'd blackmailed told his parents, and they made him cut off all communication with the man. The parents called the FBI who began watching the kid's social media. The man made good on his threat to post the kid's pictures when he quit sending more. He sent a link to one of the boy's social media pages, but in his rush the guy didn't use a proxy server. His slip-up revealed his IP address, which the Feds linked to the Arlington Internet account. We found the warehouse he was using as an office, but unfortunately it was rented with cash under an alias. The security cameras only caught a guy in a ballcap, head down. If we don't find something more, he could get away."

"No prints?"

"We got prints, but they aren't in the system."

He'd mentioned the night before that the FBI needed the help of the local cops. "So, what is your department actually doing?"

I set two bowls of oatmeal and blueberries on the table. The rich scent of coffee filling the air gave me a much needed jolt of wakefulness.

He reached for my hand, and we paused to pray for Zoe and our food before we started eating. I was glad he prayed because it still didn't feel like my prayers were doing any good, but I desperately needed God to hear and intervene.

When he finished, Michael went on, "Every victim we know of so far has been in North Texas. That's unusual because these guys have the Internet at their disposal. They operate worldwide.

"We want to know why. We're trying to see if the victims are linked in any way. They're from schools all over the area, but there maybe something else. Do they play sports? Are they on the same club league? Go to the same scouting or church camp? This case is different because it involves both boys and girls. The FBI is using all its fancy algorithms and scanning the computer's databases, but I'm trying the old-fashioned way. I'm looking through local yearbooks and trying to match faces in them to faces of the victims."

His job was demanding even without any extra work. Comprehension of what he was spending his extra time on dawned on me.

"How can you stand to look at…look at children like that?"

Michael's jaw tightened. "Remember, I can only see their faces. I try to recognize any of them. If they're real young, I memorize their features in case I spot them as an older child. We think the perp's been at this for years. The hope is if I find, say, a high school picture of a person he's got pictures of when they were younger, we might be able to track the kid down." He gave his bowl an absentminded stir, his mind obviously elsewhere.

He looked up again. "If we find any of the victims, we will see if they'll work with us. It helps the young person overcome the trauma to know they've helped lock an abuser away for life."

I got up and grabbed the coffee pot in a death grip. "Is that what'll happen to him if you find him?"

After pouring us each a mug, I sat back down and

doctored my coffee.

"Yep. From what we already know, the Feds have enough evidence from his computer to lock him away. He kept meticulous files, all coded. Having victims testify would help in the sentencing phase, however."

Michael's large hand wrapped around the mug. His knuckles whitened and I hoped the cup wouldn't shatter.

"Following all the leads might also let us discover anyone else in on this. Link him to other pedophiles we can take out, too."

I pushed my bowl away, appetite gone. I'd managed to swallow about two bites.

After a sip of coffee, I said, "I'm not letting Zoe testify. She's distraught enough as it is."

Michael's gaze shot up, meeting mine. We looked at each other a moment, then his face softened from cop-mode to dad-mode. "We don't have to talk about this now. It's way too early." He glanced at his watch. "I've gotta go."

He shoveled in a few huge spoonsful of oatmeal, got up, rinsed his bowl out, and stuck it in the dishwasher.

"Take care of my girl, and yourself, She-Girl. You should go back to bed. You look and sound terrible."

"Gee, thanks."

He kissed me on the head. "You know what I mean. I'm sorry I've got to run, but this case is super active along with everything else we've got going on."

Carrying his coffee, he headed towards the bedroom to shower, but I called out and stopped him.

"Does everyone at the department know about...?" I couldn't even say my own daughter's name.

"I'm keeping it need-to-know. Only those officers actively working the case. My assistant chief knows. She could tell I was rattled yesterday, so I let her in on what had happened." He gave me a weary smile. "Of course, I'll do my best to keep this quiet."

"Until people start finding her pictures on the Internet."

"Until then."

Chapter Seventeen

Talking In The Library

The day went downhill. My upset stomach during the evening wasn't just caused by raw emotion. Whatever virus attacked me at my lowest point kept me running to the bathroom. Not only did I have a stomach bug, but my head hurt, my throat felt raw, and talking started me coughing. An emotional and physical mess.

I dragged myself out of bed long enough to try Zoe's door a couple of times, only to be yelled at and told to go away. Christopher had been at work when all the fireworks went off the night before. When I was back in bed, he looked in on me before heading to the gym and asked if he could make me some soup.

"No, thanks, hon. I don't think I could even keep that down. My tummy is on fire."

His boyish-man's face looked at me with concern. "Is Zoe sick, too? She hasn't come out of her room."

I didn't have the strength to fill him in on what was going on yet. His dad and I would tackle that together later.

"Yeah, she doesn't feel very well, either."

"Okay," he said, with a shrug. "Call if you need anything. But otherwise, I think I'm going to hang out with the guys before work. I don't want to catch whatever you two have."

Watching as he carefully shut my bedroom door, I thought how glad I was he couldn't catch what was wrong with Zoe.

My mind finally ran out of ways to tell me what a horrible mom I was and how I'd failed my daughter, and I slept. Late in the afternoon, I got up dying of thirst. My stomach burned, my head pounded, but the thought of food sounded awful.

Passing Zoe's room on the way to the kitchen, I heard depressing music coming from behind the door. A dirty cereal bowl and an empty yogurt container sat on the kitchen counter, so I knew she'd at least come out to eat. Christopher and Michael both thought of yogurt as "sissy" food and refused to eat it.

I poured a glass of ice water and was heading back to bed when I heard my phone playing "Love Takes Time," my ringtone for Tracy. I found it on the couch from the night before.

"What's up, girlfriend?"

Her cheerful voice caused the dam to break.

"Oh, Trace. I've screwed everything up. Remember how worried I've been about Zoe doing things as bad as I used to do?"

"Yeah. What's she done? Skipped Kicker practice? Broken curfew? Some typical teenaged stuff?"

"No. It's worse. Way worse. You wouldn't believe what Michael and I just found out—"

"Whoa. Slow down. This sounds like you need to talk. I've been in Dallas all day, but I'm on my way back to town. Do you want to meet?" She paused, thinking. "Let's try out The Library." There'd been a lot of buzz about this new cocktail lounge. "I can be there in forty minutes or so. I hear it's great."

Agreeing to meet, I headed upstairs. I still felt pretty crappy, but at least I didn't have *that* particular intestinal issue. After a quick rinse-off, I pulled my hair into a messy updo, wiggled into some skinny jeans, and, because it was blazing hot outside, flip-flops and a light-cotton shirt. Slugging down more cold and cough liquid so I wouldn't sound like a grizzly bear or bark like a seal, I considered doubling the dose. But I didn't want to be groggy while driving. Instead, I popped a couple of extra aspirin for my pounding head.

On the way, I stopped outside Zoe's door. "I'm going out with Tracy for a bit. Are you going to be okay?"

"Yeah, just peachy. I'm in here trying to choose which Ivy League school to attend now that I'm a famous porn star."

"Oh, Zo." My heart pinched.

"Go on, Mom. Go. It's not like *I'll* ever have a life again."

"Sweetie, I'm happy to stay home with you. Do you want to talk?" I placed a hand against her door and laid my forehead against the wood. It felt blissfully cool.

"No!" her voice screamed back at me from inside. "I don't want to talk. I don't want to do anything. Ever. Go away and leave me alone."

Leaning against her door, I felt even weaker than I'd been a few moments before. "I won't be long. Call if you need me." I heard her throw herself on the bed and start sobbing.

Rooted to the spot, I debated what to do. Throwing myself on the bed and crying sounded good, but that wouldn't help me or my daughter. I'd been there and done that for the last twenty-four hours.

Maybe Tracy was right. Talking might help me get things in perspective. She and I had seen each other through plenty of rough times.

Grabbing my purse, I headed to the garage.

Early evening was too late in the day for coffee, and fast food joints would be packed, so I guessed that's why Tracy suggested a bar, even though that was definitely not our normal venue for hanging out. I'd heard about The Library. Who hadn't? But I'd never been there. It was in a town about twenty minutes away, and unlike most joints in Graitney, it catered to a more mature crowd, specializing in cocktails rather than beer.

Until recently, our town's watering holes were populated by farmers and oilfield workers. Now, a few places served margaritas with their Mexican food. Some offered wine. Nothing really catered to adults who wanted to have a quiet conversation. Plus, The Library had the added advantage of being out of the our city limits. There was less of a chance of running into someone I knew while I spilled my guts.

Tracy was thoughtful that way.

I looked up the address and let my phone's GPS talk to me as I drove. The calm British voice telling me where to turn was soothing. I wished it could tell me how to get out of this mess.

In no time, I'd arrived and found a place to park in front of the historical courthouse that stood in the center of the city square. Tracy was waiting on the sidewalk.

"Cute top," she said when I got out of the car, then she did a double take. "Are you okay? You look kind of…tired."

"I know. This morning, Michael told me I looked awful. I'm sick and wouldn't even be out of bed, but I can't stand being in that house with my thoughts a minute longer. Thank goodness you called. I promise not to breathe on you."

She laughed. "As if I haven't already been exposed to whatever it is."

Tracy had told me long ago that the first year of teaching you catch everything the kids have, then your immune system kicks in, and you become resilient to most everything. She was one of the toughest people I knew, not just physically but mentally and emotionally.

She'd been through a lot in life.

Tracy lost her folks when she was young and wanted nothing more than to be married to a Prince Charming and be a mom. The marriage she'd gotten, but neither the kids nor the fairytale followed.

The Library filled the top story of a hardware store built in 1888. The door to the street was unmarked, but she knew where to go. It felt as if we were entering a Speakeasy. We climbed the steep staircase. Walking inside was like walking into an old reading room. Persian rugs muted our steps on the hardwood floor. Between the large windows that faced the courthouse and those along the side street, the walls held shelves of hardback books salvaged from some demolished library. The artwork was traditional European-style: busts tucked among the tomes and pastoral scenes in heavy frames.

We were early enough to get a table looking out one of the windows. The long wine-colored velvet drapes stood open, showcasing the nighttime square. White lights in the trees twinkled against a cloudy backdrop.

A bar stretched along the back of the small club. The mixologist – Tracy corrected me when I'd called the lady a bartender – asked what we wanted to drink. Tracy ordered a fancy drink off the menu. The lilac-colored concoction came in a martini glass with a sprig of fresh lavender balanced on the rim. It smelled heavenly.

The mixologist turned to me. "What can I make you?"

"I'll take a ginger ale, please," I said, thinking about my upset stomach.

Tracy made a face. "That's like going to the Louvre and thumbing through a coloring book. Try a drink off the menu."

The bartender, a woman in her late twenties with a brick-red pixie haircut and a spider web tattoo on her neck, laughed. "How about I mix that ginger ale with something? I can make most anything you want."

I looked at Tracy. "Michael and I don't drink."

"You and I used to." She laughed.

"Yeah, but we'd get smashed on cheap wine coolers."

I looked back at the list of drinks. "I don't know what any of this is."

"My head hurts just thinking about those old days," Tracy laughed.

"Here's an idea," the mixologist said, grabbing a fat copper mug out of a refrigerator. "If you like ginger, you'll love a Moscow Mule."

She mixed together a couple of things and handed me the frosty mug. I took a tentative sip while Tracy gave her a credit card to start a tab. It had been years since I'd drunk alcohol, and I was afraid it would be too strong, but the drink tasted of ginger and lime.

I smiled at the young woman. "You're right. It's good."

We went back to our table. Thankfully, it was in a little niche at the far end of the room, so no one was within earshot.

"Okay," Tracy said after we got seated, "spill it. What's up?"

Good thing my back was to the room because tears welled up in my eyes. Taking a hasty gulp, I blinked rapidly, feeling pressure in the bridge of my nose. I settled myself for a second, then launched into the story. Tracy didn't interrupt as I told everything that had happened the day before.

As I talked, a waiter appeared at my elbow with

another drink. He took away my empty mug, and I started in on the new icy-cold Moscow Mule. It tasted blissfully refreshing. I'd been parched all day. It didn't help that the antihistamines I'd been taking made my mouth feel like I had been noshing on cotton balls.

"Have you ever heard of anything worse?" I demanded when I finished but didn't let Tracy answer. "What kind of mother is so oblivious that her daughter is making soft-core porn in her bedroom and she doesn't know it? I always thought we were close. I thought Zoe could come to me with anything. That she *would* come to me with anything."

"This all happened in what? The last couple of months?" Tracy asked raising an eyebrow with a tiny diamond stud. "How could you have known if she hid it from you? Teenagers excel at that."

"I *did* know something was wrong, but everyone kept saying it's normal for teens to be secretive. But I know Zoe. I should have done something. I should have made her talk to me."

"Like you can make teenagers do anything they don't want to do." Tracy's eyes crinkled over the rim of her drink. "Trust me, I know. Sometimes I feel like I'm mom to dozens of them."

"Poor Zoe's the victim here. I've failed her in the worst way possible. It's a shame she didn't have a mother who could have stopped this in time."

"Like anyone could have."

"It's too late for recriminations, anyway." I played with a slice of lime I'd fished from my drink. "What's done is done, but Zoe's right. How is her life not ruined? That filth is on the Internet for heaven's sake. Everyone and their Cocker spaniel can see what's happened to her. She'll never get away from it. *We'll* never get away from it."

Tracy put her hand on mine. "Relax, Sheena. I've never seen you this stressed. Zoe needs you to be strong. Now more than ever."

"I know. I just don't know how to do it. I'm a ball of nerves. Can't eat. Can't sleep. And now sick to boot."

I took another swig. "But the drink was a good idea. This is the best I've felt in days." I shook my head at the absurdity of the statement. "At least, physically. Emotionally, I'm a wreck."

"I'm sorry. I know it's rough."

I stared into my drink for a moment, then looked at Tracy. "Let's talk about you. How are you doing? How's life as a single woman?"

Tracy smiled. "Parts are good. I've started the process to get certified as a foster parent."

"What? That's a great idea, Tracy. You'd be a wonderful foster mom."

Excitement sparked in her dark eyes. "Thanks. I hope it works out. I'm tired of wallowing in self-pity. I want my life to make a difference."

"Trace, your life already makes a difference to so many kids."

"Thanks." She sent me a grateful look. "I want to impact someone who *really* needs me. I'm especially interested in older children; they're harder to place. Who knows? If everything goes well, I may get to care for one I can eventually adopt."

She looked the happiest I'd seen her in a long time. Tracy put on a brave face, but she'd paid a heavy emotional toll ever since it became clear her marriage wouldn't make it.

We continued to talk, cozy in our nook while rain blurred the lights outside the window and the volume in the lounge grew louder. I slowed down on the cocktails. Tracy didn't. I declined a drink when the waiter came around for the umpteenth time but then wished I'd asked for water. Since the mixologist created one cocktail at a time, the line at the bar was long, and I didn't want to get up and wait in it, so I went without.

"I didn't have any idea all that was going on," I said after Tracy admitted Rod had been unfaithful more than once.

Her cheeks washed with a pink nearly the color of her hair, but she laughed out loud. "Thank God! Do you have any idea how hard I worked to make our marriage look *normal*? I kept hoping things would work out, and, for some reason, I didn't want my friends to hate the heel I'd married."

Suddenly, her eyes brimmed. "I was such an idiot for so long." Tracy brushed angrily at the tears. "I won't be so gullible again, believe me."

She continued to unload years' worth of garbage from an unhealthy marriage. Finally, when she slowed down a little, I glanced at my phone and noticed it was almost ten-thirty. "We'd better go. I hate to leave Zoe alone this long. I'm afraid she might do something to hurt herself."

"Oh, Sheena." Tracy's hand flew to her face, covering her mouth. Her eyebrows drew together over frightened eyes. "Don't even say that! Words have power, you know."

Her emotions flipped and she giggled. "Thanks for listening. I guess I'd bottled all that junk up for a long time. Buying you a couple of drinks is much cheaper than a shrink."

"I'm happy to listen. You've always been there for me."

"I'll be praying for Zoe and your whole family," Tracy said, getting up.

"Thanks. We need it." I stood up. A rush of lightheadedness washed over me. Gone in an instant.

But Tracy stumbled a little and had to grab the table for support.

"Are you, okay?" I asked. How many drinks had she gone through?

How many had I?

"Yeah." She grinned, cocking her head. The curl of diamond studs along her ear caught the light and glinted. "I'm fine."

The room swayed and I felt woozy. I needed to eat.

A knife-stab of pain tore through my gut.

"I really do appreciate having you to talk to." I gathered up my purse and phone. "Zoe's shut me out. Michael's working night and day to bring this sicko to justice, and I hate to even think about what Christopher will say when he finds out what's happened. He dotes on his baby sister. This isn't the kind of thing I want to share with most of my friends. Even Kara."

"You always have me." Tracy smiled and for some reason our high school selves flashed through my mind.

Tracy, part of the in-crowd, already had a date to senior prom with the star pitcher on the baseball team. Tall, skinny, and shy, I had no plans to attend. I'd barely ever spoken to a boy, let alone gone on a real date. Without making a huge deal about it, Tracy talked her guy into rounding up some of his buddies to go with her girlfriends as a group to prom. I had the best night of my teenaged life and amazingly found out that not all guys were attracted to busty girls. I met John who was a "leg man." He became

my first boyfriend and slowly brought me out of my
protective shell.

I had Tracy to thank for that.

Chapter Eighteen

What Happened?

Present

Opening my eyes, I saw the most beautiful sight in the world – my kids and husband walking into the room. They should have seemed happy to see me. They didn't. Something was wrong. They looked scared. My brain struggled. Thoughts slugged to the surface like bubbles in hot August tar. Thick. Slow.

Where was I? I looked around. I was in a hospital room.

Why?

Zoe, Christopher, and Michael crept to my bed, as if afraid of breaking me. They crowded in close to touch me. Smiles didn't mask the worry in their eyes.

"It's okay, Sheena," Michael said. Strain cracked his normally calm voice. "You're going to be okay." He stroked my hand, the one with a little plastic thing snapped to the finger.

The other side had an IV attached. Zoe's hand softly covered the tape.

"What happened?" My voice sounded croaky, weak. Every part of me hurt.

My mind frantically searched its memory banks. Empty. Zilch. A blank nothingness, giant and black. A void waiting to draw me back down into it.

Palpable fear radiated off my family.

Christopher laid a hand on my leg. "You were in a car accident, Mom."

"The people in the other car are okay," Michael answered the question before my sluggish brain formed it.

I studied their faces, desperate for reassurance. None of them met my gaze. They stared at something behind me that beeped. A monitor? Zoe's eyes were nearly swollen shut from crying. I couldn't remember ever seeing her look this devastated.

Could I? My mind, always so sharp and reliable, failed me. Panic pressed down on me, far heavier than the cotton hospital blanket.

"What happened?"

"Not now, Sheena," Michael said, his take-charge tone back.

A nurse who'd been hovering in the background

stepped forward.

"That's right, Mrs. McKenzie. You need to rest. The doctors worked hard to keep you alive. Let's not hinder their efforts."

"Alive?"

Michael gripped down on my hand. "CareFlight brought you here. They revived you three times."

"I died?" Why couldn't I remember any of this?

Zoe sobbed and turned around, lurching for the tissues on the counter. My husband shrugged, looking stricken.

"Everyone's been praying, Mom." Hope flared in Christopher's nearly-adult face. "Everyone from your Bible study, the church, even people that read about the accident on social media and passed it on. People around the world we don't even know are praying."

The anxiety lifted. Everything would be okay.

A tawny lion, mane black and bristling, padded past in the hallway. Silent. Transparent. Glowing. The huge feline paused at the door. I stared at him, and, somehow, he didn't seem out of place. His inky black eyes looked deep into mine.

That made perfect sense, even though nothing else did.

Chapter Nineteen

Broken Brain

Four Days Later

"Now that you are stabilized, Mrs. McKenzie," a man who'd introduced himself as Dr. Kraus said, staring down at the tablet in his hand, "we can finally run some tests."

So grave for such a young-looking man. His youthful, rounded face made me feel every one of my forty-three years. That and my banged-up body.

"Thought I'd been through a ton of tests already," I tried for a humorous tone and grinned at Michael, hoping to keep things light. But both men looked deadly serious.

Dr. Kraus contemplated me through curious brown eyes. "We've done standard CBC, electrolyte, cortisol levels, blood and urine cultures, MRI, etc. We are trying to determine the cause of the continuing anemia and low blood pressure. You presented in shock with severe dehydration, which would exacerbate the hypotension, as would a Vasovagal reaction – a condition where a healthy person temporarily develops low blood pressure, even fainting that can be brought on by vomiting."

The doctor's words blurred into a blah, blah, blah. He seemed so ill at ease I felt an urge to comfort him.

I looked at Michael to see if he was following all this. My poor brain wasn't up to it yet. Thinking hurt. Even normal words didn't exactly click and make sense. The accident left me bruised and sore with a jagged gash on my thigh. The broken brain was worse. They'd ruled out traumatic brain injury from the accident. Rather, my blood pressure and oxygen levels having been extremely low caused the memory problems. At least, that's what I think he was talking about.

Michael had finally told me I'd been driving at the time of the accident and was lucky to have survived. Everything had a dreamlike quality to it.

Even that devastating information.

The doctor's gaze shifted back to my chart and his tone dropped. "We aren't privy to information contained in the toxicology report, but I understand that now you are conscious, Mrs. McKenzie, the sheriff's department would like to talk to you."

The urge to comfort the doctor evaporated. Sheriff?

Michael spoke up, "I've made arrangements for our

lawyer to be here this afternoon."

Lawyer? The talk of a tox screen I'd overheard had to do with the other driver, didn't it? Why would they have to talk to me? I couldn't remember anything about the accident. I'd be no help.

I cut my eyes towards Michael, but his gaze seemed riveted on the doctor's tablet, as if it held the answer to everything.

As soon as the doctor left the room, I pounced. "What's going on? What's this about the sheriff? You told me the people in the other car are okay. I thought *they* were at fault."

He shifted uncomfortably. An awful thought bubbled to the surface of my mind

"Are you telling me I was at fault?" Thoughts popped up faster. "Am I at fault? It's bad if I need a lawyer. Do we have a lawyer?"

Michael got up, walked over, and stood beside me. He towered over the hospital bed, and I realized how intimidating it would be to be on the opposite side of the law from him.

He ran a finger along my face, tucking a strand of hair behind my ear. I couldn't remember seeing him look so sad – a tender, aching sadness that pierced my heart.

"I'd hoped to have this conversation once you are home, She-Girl, but it seems you need to stay longer for them to run the extra tests."

"What have you all been keeping from me?" Scary new thoughts simmered in my mind demanding answers. I felt twitchy, out of control as if surging with electricity. "I caused the accident, didn't I?"

His gaze linked with mine, questioning. "Do you remember something? Tell me. Tell me about that night."

Ever since I'd first regained consciousness, I'd had only hazy, sporadic memories. Some had to be hallucinations, although they made perfect sense at the time. A lion. My dead grandparents. Floating dictionaries. So many things that couldn't have really been there. I couldn't remember them all. Not only did my brain not work well in the present, everything around the accident was a gigantic blank.

I had no sense of time either. It grew and shrank. Thundering past or jerking moment by moment forward.

I'd slowly recalled what happened to Zoe. But when I asked Michael about the investigation or anything else going on with the family, he put me off and told me not to worry. He meant well, but as I got stronger, not knowing anything drove me crazy.

The accident was a taboo subject, as well. He knew I couldn't remember much after talking to Tracy on the phone. By the eager look on his face now, he obviously hoped my memory was coming back.

Michael raised an eyebrow waiting for me to speak. Not only did I want to please him, but everything in me longed for answers. I tried to hold on to an image that was as insubstantial as a mirage.

"All day, I'd been super upset about everything happening with Zoe, and I didn't feel good to boot. I'd been sick, staying in bed, yet antsy, anxious to get out of the house. So, Tracy suggested.... She called me, I think. Maybe I called her."

I paused listening to Tracy's ringtone play in my head.

Feeling Michael's gaze on me, I snapped back to the moment. "Anyway, she suggested we go out and talk. Then...Then what?" I huffed in frustration. "It's a blur. I'm not sure why we were at that place out of town."

"The Library."

"Yeah. That's it. We were there quite a while. Maybe. I'm not sure. Perhaps."

"Drinking?"

Visions of a lavender drink, a spider web tattoo, lights around the courthouse square blurred by the rain flashed like sparks and just as quickly were gone.

"No. I haven't had a drink in years." When I met Michael, I liked the fact that he didn't drink. In his job, he'd seen where the abuse of alcohol could lead. I'd been glad to leave that not so great part of my life behind.

I tasted lime and ginger.

"Maybe." I nodded, then shook my head. "Yeah, I think so, but I'm not sure."

Michael was biting his lip. An angry green light flared in the depths of his eyes, but it quickly disappeared, replaced by love and concern. Had I seen it at all or was it just another thing I'd imagined? I concentrated on remembering anything else.

"We talked about Zoe. Lots." Just the fragment of the memory of that conversation made my stomach burn.

Pausing, I grasped for more. "Tracy talked about bad marriage stuff... I think. But maybe that was a different conversation."

I stared up at the acoustical tiles, searching, but nothing else came. I looked at Michael again. "I'm sorry. There's nothing. Nothing else. It's so maddening. How can I not know what I did?"

"Did you drive there together?"

This struck me as an odd question. But why was it odd?

"No, I don't think we did, but...." Something was there, just out of reach.

It felt like whatever it was hovered just outside my peripheral vision, and if I turned my head fast enough I could see it. Of course, my head hurt way too much to go jerking it around. Besides it was a memory I was after, not these fleeting images.

Michael's voice brought my wandering mind back to the conversation. "You were driving home…"

"Okay. So, I was driving home from The Library when the accident happened?" I asked. "Really? I don't remember that at all."

Shutting my eyes in frustration, I tried to recollect anything else about that night. The few brief glimpses I'd shared vanished. They refused to come back. I might as well be trying to read a scrap of paper immersed in a tub of dye. A deep black nothingness. Opening them, I saw Michael studying my face. He looked seriously worried.

Nothing made sense. "You said that the accident was Tuesday night and today is Saturday, right? It doesn't seem possible. How can I remember almost nothing of the last four days?"

"It's okay. The doctor said all this is completely normal. In fact, you are doing better than anyone expected."

Michael laid his hand on my shoulder, I assumed to comfort me and let me know it was okay that I couldn't remember, but he kept talking. "I take it you were driving Tracy home. Perhaps she'd had too much to drink."

I looked up confused. "Why do you say that?"

"She was in the car with you."

"No. That's not possible, because I'm so badly hurt, and she isn't hurt at all."

Now, Michael looked confused. "What do you mean?"

"I'm mean she's just fine."

"Tracy's fine?"

"Yeah. She came to visit me a couple of times. She looks great."

"Oh, She-Girl," Michael gripped down harder on my shoulder, as if it was his police baton. "I'm so sorry, but you need to know. You've got to know the truth. Tracy didn't…She didn't make it."

"Didn't make it where?"

Chapter Twenty

The Awful Truth

"She-Girl…," Michael said, "Tracy didn't make it. She didn't survive."

I stared at him, uncomprehending.

"Tracy died." The words coming out of his mouth sounded as if he'd dragged them up from the grave itself.

"Died?" I repeated with a chuff. "She can't have. I saw her with my own eyes. She was her normal silly self."

"She died in the accident."

It couldn't be true. Tracy couldn't be dead. No one was more vibrant or full of life.

"She died in the accident?" My mind refused to believe what my mouth parroted. I frowned at Michael sure I'd misunderstood.

His eyes didn't lie. Their usually intense greyish-green

looked bleak and cold like mold.

I shook my head. "But she came to visit me, here. I remember that."

"You saw a lot of things. Lions. Your grandparents. You told me about it. Between the brain trauma and the painkillers, you've been pretty out of it. Tracy was just another hallucination." He looked incredibly sad, as if what he was saying was true.

"She can't be!" I shook my head frantically, even while my mouth formed words I didn't believe. "I killed my oldest friend?"

For the first time in days, thoughts came thick and furious.

It's not true! I can't believe it. I won't believe it...

Yet, I knew it. Down in my deepest, most terrifying, nightmare-producing fears, I knew it.

It had the deathly ring of truth.

Michael looked at me, the sorrow born of years of delivering bad news written in every line of his face.

I screamed at him, "No! No! No!"

My thoughts warred. Tracy's dead. She's not. She's dead. She's not. Suddenly, I had no control, not of my mind or my body.

Keening and wailing, harsh animal sounds, filled the room. My arms and legs jerked as my body tried to curl into a fetal position, yanking against the IV tethering me.

My legs bound by sheets and a bulky bandage. Electrodes on my chest pinned me in place.

Trapped. No way to escape the horror of his words. Deep body-spasm cries rose from my gut, tore through my lungs, and out a raw throat. A pressure, like the weight of every tragedy that had ever happened since the world began, crushed my chest. Yet, the howls continued.

The shaking started so violently it rattled the bed.

I can't survive this. I can't. I can't... I don't want to.

Dr. Kraus rushed back in, a nurse in tow. "Start a sedative. STAT!"

Chapter Twenty-One

Numb

"Hardy, Samuel Hardy," the short, confident man with thick, salt and pepper hair said, extending his hand.

I had slumped docile while given a spit bath and put in a clean hospital gown for the occasion. The room contained no mirror. I didn't even want to know what I looked like. Didn't care. Didn't care about anything.

Never would again.

Tracy was dead. I'd killed her. The truth of those words thrummed over and over in my mind like car tires on wet pavement.

We shook hands, and a detached part of my brain noticed the attorney had a firm handshake. A pet-peeve of mine was men giving women limp-fish shakes, as if our hands would break if they were as robust with us as with men. He also gave me a direct, caring look out of thoughtful, hazel eyes. Even through the numbness, he'd managed to make me trust him.

Quite a trick and a good trait in a lawyer, especially one who held my fate in his hands.

"I understand from your husband that you don't recall the events surrounding or following the accident, is that correct?"

I blinked yes. Words were too difficult to manage.

"Let me give you a little information pertinent to your case." He settled himself on a molded-plastic chair. Michael perched on the edge of the chair hide-a-bed.

The attorney continued, "At the time of the accident, the responding officer did not suspect you of driving under the influence. Which is fortunate, or you would have been placed under arrest immediately, restrained – as in handcuffed to the bed – with a guard posted outside the door during your entire hospitalization."

It didn't seem impossible that things could be worse. A shiver of dread ran through my body. But maybe they could.

"However," he paused.

Icy tendrils crept around my numb heart.

"As a fatality was involved, it is standard procedure for law enforcement to investigate." His gaze flicked to Michael who steadfastly looked at the wall opposite him but nodded slightly.

"In your case, they've now decided they do have probable cause to believe you were under the influence of alcohol or a controlled substance at the time of the accident."

"I've never taken illegal drugs." The words shot out of my mouth before I'd even formed them.

Then I remembered I'd been drinking with Tracy. What if we'd gotten smashed? Like we had when we were stupid college kids. I had no idea how drunk I might have been. Could I have done something worse? Hard to believe, but I still couldn't believe I'd killed one of my best friends, either.

Hardy went on as if people shouted at him all the time. "Based on what they discovered, the police obtained a pocket warrant from a judge for intoxication manslaughter. I expect you to be placed under arrest. You will be magistrated by a judge, bond will be set, and you should be able to go home to await indictment by a grand jury."

The head of the bed was tilted up, raising me to a semi-sitting position, but at his words I scooched further down into the blankets.

Disappearing would have been preferable.

"As this case is a second-degree felony, proper protocol was followed. The police had the hospital pull a separate blood sample because those for law enforcement are handled, packaged, and analyzed differently than medical ones. The blood was shipped to a DPS lab for testing. Here in Dallas it first goes to a lab in Garland to test for alcohol content, then on to the crime lab in Austin to be tested for drugs."

It seemed pointless to tell him again that I'd never done drugs.

"The time it takes to get the results can vary, but it could take anywhere from months to years because the lab is so back-logged. We will have to go through the necessary discovery procedures once the results are available."

As the lawyer talked, Michael stared at the wall, rocking gently back and forth. He knew all this, of course.

Hardy explained more about what I'd be charged with and what to expect after the meeting with the Sheriff's department, how the case would proceed, and what he would handle. Even though this was undoubtedly the most important information I'd ever received in my life, I couldn't absorb what he said.

As Michael told him at the beginning, I wasn't really "with it" yet. My mind still played tricks on me. Not as much as it had initially, but I was far from normal. The sedative they'd given me didn't help.

Trying to remember the night of the accident only brought up a big black nothing. As far as I could tell, I wasn't hallucinating as much, but my mind responded like a microwave stuck on defrost. Nothing near full-power. On top of that, hearing the news about Tracy sent me into a tailspin from which I doubted I'd recover and, frankly, didn't see any reason to. I may never have taken illegal drugs, but prescription ones to numb the raging pain sounded like a fine idea.

He finished talking and looked at me as if expecting an answer. I had none. A Graitney Gazette headline floated in front of my eyes, "Convicted felon Sheena McKenzie brings kale salad to High Kicker function."

No chance of that. What could I say? My life was screwed.

Samuel Hardy had explained that I was facing an intoxication manslaughter charge since someone died in the accident. With a second-degree felony, I could receive two to twenty years of prison time and up to a $10,000 fine.

No more school events. No events of any kind. Chances were my kids were going to grow up and leave home with their mom locked away in the state pen.

"The upshot, Sheena," Michael watched me, worry furrowing his brow, "is to let Mr. Hardy do the talking when the detective from the Sheriff's Department questions you about the accident. Got that?"

"No problem. I can't remember anything anyway."

I'd no more than said this when there was a knock at

the door. Michael called for them to come in. A petite woman in black pants and a white top, a Dallas County Sheriff's department badge clipped to her belt, opened the door and strode into the room. She wore her dark brown hair short and slicked back.

"Hi, Chief McKenzie." She walked over to Michael. "I'm glad to see you again. Just sorry it's at such a difficult time."

He stood up. The female officer's head didn't quite reach his shoulder.

"Don't worry about it, Detective Hernandez. You're just doing your job. Laura, this is my wife, Sheena McKenzie, and our attorney, Samuel Hardy."

The detective shook both our hands. She too had a nice firm grip. There was no nonsense about the woman. The detective immediately asked me a question about the night of the accident.

Hardy jumped right in, as if afraid I'd forget not to answer. "Mrs. McKenzie has been advised to invoke her Fifth Amendment right to remain silent."

"Not hard to do seeing as how I can't remember anything," I mumbled.

Both Michael and Hardy threw me evil looks.

"All right," I said, making the zipped lips gesture.

Detective Hernandez cracked a sad smile. "Mrs. McKenzie wasn't cited at the scene because the responding

officer saw no evidence that alcohol was involved, but
Chief McKenzie has asked us to dot all our i's and cross all
our t's."

I glared at Michael, who ignored me. There might not
have been all this legal trouble if my husband hadn't
intervened? It was just like him to have his own wife held
under tighter scrutiny than any other person, not less.

Detective Hernandez saw the look I'd sent my
husband and added, "Which we would do in a fatality case
anyway."

I crossed my arms, mad at her now, not Michael.

She went on. "A judge issued a probable cause warrant
to have Mrs. McKenzie's blood analyzed for alcohol, and
since stomach contents were also present, we are testing
them for drug use as well."

I wanted to shout at her that I'd been sick and
upchucking before the accident, but I'd zipped my lips
shut.

"Are you placing her under arrest, now?" the lawyer
asked.

"No, you can surrender yourself upon discharge,"
Detective Hernandez said to me, her eyes firmly on my
husband.

I knew him well enough to notice the muscle bulging
in his jaw, his teeth clenched hard. This had to be a
nightmare for him.

"They won't release her until they've run more tests."
His soft voice sounded as brittle as I'd ever heard. "It may
still take a few days."

"No problem. All of us are handling this as quietly as
we can." Detective Hernandez looked truly apologetic.
"Again, Chief, I'm so sorry your family is in this position.
I really am."

I felt bad for being ready to shoot the messenger.
Detective Hernandez hadn't gotten me into this mess. I
had. I was the only one to blame. She nodded toward me
and Hardy before leaving the room.

If I'd thought I couldn't feel any worse, I was wrong.
The sagging shoulders and look of humiliation on
Michael's face as he watched a fellow law enforcement
officer leave after telling his wife she was going to be
arrested plummeted me to an all-time low.

Chapter Twenty-Two

Picking A Fight

The next week went by in an anesthetized blur of tests and somber family visits. I cried and slept a lot. During the long stay at the hospital, I couldn't wait to get home to my own bed, my own kids, my own cats.

My own husband I wasn't as certain about.

Michael came to see me every day, but he looked progressively worse. The purple smudges under his eyes appeared drawn on with permanent marker, as did the new lines etched on his brow. His sideburns turned silver seemingly overnight and a smattering of the light strands flashed throughout his dark hair.

He'd aged ten years in the last two weeks.

With what was going on with me and Zoe, it wasn't surprising.

He acted completely sweet and supportive, but I knew he had to be furious with me. The chief of police's wife under arrest for intoxication manslaughter. Who could blame him?

Perversely, I kept trying to force anger out of him. To get him to show me how mad he was at me. As if getting him to yell at me like I deserved could somehow make me feel better. I couldn't beat myself up any more than I had already. I needed him to do it. To tell me what a rotten person I was.

It was later than normal on a Friday night when Michael made the long drive into the city to see me. He shuffled into the room like a tired old man.

"Honey, you don't have to come see me every night. It's late. You should be home sleeping."

He didn't answer, just came over and kissed the top of my head before collapsing onto the hard-plastic chair.

"Bad day?" I asked.

He scrubbed the back of his hand across his jaw. "No more than usual."

Since the accident, we hadn't talked about anything going on with the Zoe investigation. He shut me down whenever I tried to bring it up.

"I hate that I've made things even harder on you." I watched him carefully, knowing the anger had to be just beneath the surface. I couldn't stand myself for what I'd done to our family and to Michael's reputation. How could he?

"It's fine, She-Girl. You had an accident. Remember, we talked about this. Until we know definitively what your BAC was, let's assume it was an accident."

"Some accident. I shouldn't have driven after I'd been drinking. I can't remember anything about it. What if I had ten drinks? Or worse! What if I did something totally nuts like drugs? I can't remember any of it." I chortled like a crazy woman, but my voice broke on a sob.

"It really doesn't matter if I only had one drink. I shouldn't have been driving."

He stayed quiet, staring at the dusty tops of his boots.

"Isn't that what we tell the kids? Isn't that what your department preaches?"

Michael shifted, looking uncomfortable. "Sheena, it's been a long day. Can we not go there?"

"That's what you'd like, isn't it? Not to go there. That's what we'd all like: never having to be here – facing this. But we are here in this mess, and it's my fault. We should be concentrating on helping Zoe, and instead it's all about me and the fact that I killed my best friend and might go to jail for it."

My voice got louder and Michael shot a nervous glance towards the nurse's station, but I couldn't stop myself.

"Just say it. Just say it out loud. You hate me."

"I don't hate –"

"You can't even look at me!"

He finally looked up. "Calm down. It isn't good for you to—"

"Good for me?" I barked out a hysterical snort. "Good for me? Like I care."

The night-shift nurse hurried into the room.

"Sheena," Michael said, standing up, "you're tired and upset."

"Yeah, and that's totally ridiculous. What could I have to be upset about?"

"I'll see you tomorrow," he mumbled hurrying from the room.

I took grim pleasure in knowing I'd been right; he couldn't stand me. For the first time in twenty years of marriage, he'd left without giving me a kiss.

Like turning off a gas burner, the anger that flared so hot for a moment disappeared. Familiar icy despair rushed back.

The nurse reached for the IV line. "Here's some more sedative, Mrs. McKenzie."

I rolled onto my side as best I could, pulling the covers under my chin.

"No need," I said in a believably calm voice. "I'm fine now."

Chapter Twenty-Three

Homecoming

The hospital discharged me the day after our fight. Michael picked me up. As he started the car, I braced myself against a flood of fear that didn't come. I'd assumed that after such a horrific accident, I'd be afraid to be back in a car. But I guess one of the blessings of not remembering something was actually not remembering it. Everything seemed perfectly normal until I thought about where we were headed.

Michael drove me to the sheriff's department so I could turn myself in. He called it surrendering. What a horrible word.

I was grateful Detective Hernandez hadn't publically arrested me at the hospital. The isolation of an office at the sheriff's department was awful enough.

It wasn't like I was a flight risk. I was too weak. It had taken numerous transfusions to get my numbers back in the normal range once they'd found and treated the bleeding ulcer that was the underlying reason for my blood loss and the reason for the horrible pain in my gut. I left the hospital with a bunch of prescriptions and cautions about taking it easy. That suited me just fine because I had no desire to see anyone ever again. The large bandage on my leg made walking awkward, too.

Michael worked some magic allowing me to immediately appear before a judge with only my lawyer at my side. After he set bail, I left the courthouse through a back door, clinging to Michael's arm. A physical and emotional cripple. Being able to do all this on our own time and privately was in deference to Michael's position within the law enforcement community. I felt ashamed but grateful.

Zoe waited for me at home.

One surprise blessing from my car accident was it cleared the air between Zoe and me. At least, on the surface. There is something to be said for a mom doing something worse than her daughter to get them back on level footing. Besides that, the whole family had been sure I was going to die. Zoe's fear of losing her mom seemed to be stronger than anger at me for losing her dance teacher. Everyone, even the hospital staff, thought I was going to die. There didn't seem to be a good explanation of why I hadn't.

When I thought of what I'd done, I wished I had.

Zoe helped me into the house. Something wonderful happened as I walked into my own home after being gone so long. Not happiness. I doubted I'd ever feel that again. But a sense of comfort, like an animal returning to the safety of its den, enveloped me.

Michael nodded toward a mass of blankets and pillows. "Before he went to work, Christopher made you a nest on the couch, so you can watch TV while you recuperate." He set down one of the bags he'd been carrying. "You won't have to climb the stairs, if you aren't up to it."

The feeling thinned a little. Did Michael not want me back in bed with him? Was he that mad at me? It took too much energy to think about. Instead, I concentrated on feeling grateful for my son's efforts.

He'd placed a card table alongside the sofa. It held the various remotes, tissues, an insulated water bottle, a stack of books, one of magazines, a bowl of fruit, and three bags of Cheetos. My favorite indulgence.

Zoe pulled back a soft throw blanket, arranged the pillows, and waited for me to settle in.

The undeserved kindness of my family brought the familiar knot of grief and shame to my throat. I had no tears left to cry over what I'd done, but the raw aching sadness never left.

"What do I smell?" I asked, gingerly lowering myself onto the couch.

I swung my legs up and lay back. Immediately, Anne, my gorgeous cat jumped up and sat on my lap. She looked at me with the breed's trademark blue eyes and I began petting her long silky fur. Ragdolls are cuddly cats and right then I couldn't be more appreciative. Her paws opened and closed rhythmically in kitty contentment.

"Chicken and cheese?" I sniffed the air. "And what's that Mexican spice?"

Simple words I'd known forever escaped me, but as soon as someone told me they'd be back in place, just as if I'd never struggled with them at all. The traumatic brain injury specialist who'd seen me at the hospital said my brain was busy literally rewiring damaged pathways.

"Cumin," Michael supplied.

"Cumin," I echoed. How could I have forgotten something I cooked with all the time?

"Yep, King Ranch casserole," Zoe said. "Just like Nana used to make."

For the first time since the accident, food sounded remotely good to me. I'd lost ten pounds.

"Did you make it, sweetie?" I asked, sending Zoe a thankful look. She knew it was one of my favorites.

"No, Cecilia from church brought it," Michael answered. "Dolores brought a frozen lasagna. Gabby made enough pasta salad for ten of us. Church people, neighbors, cops have brought things by all week. The fridge and freezer are stuffed, and they have an online calendar with even more people signed up."

From the doorway he added, "Ida made her infamous strawberry shortcake."

Michael looked at me, waiting for me to laugh at the old family joke. No one could make rock-hard shortcake and be more obliviously proud than Ida Foster. Forcing my lips to curl, I tried to hold a smile. It hadn't dawned on me that people would be doing nice things for us.

An intense mixture of gratefulness and guilt rushed over me, followed by a keen awareness that everyone knew what had happened. They all knew I killed Tracy. Suddenly, I wasn't the least bit hungry.

Not understanding how awful I felt, Zoe added. "Look at those gorgeous flowers from the High Kickers."

The largest bouquet I'd ever seen sat in the middle of the dining room table. Tall orange Calla Lilly's and long-stem yellow roses towered over peonies and other smaller flowers in the same colors. Nestled in the middle were several creamy white gardenias. The strong smell of dinner mingled with their distinctive sweet scent. Noticing that made me faintly nauseated, like nearly everything seemed to do lately.

"There's about a thousand cards here for you, too," Zoe said going to the table and fanning through a huge stack of mail by the flowers.

"Don't they know what I did?" my voice came out squeaky. "Do they know about Tracy?"

Her funeral had been held while I was in the hospital. I'd sent her Aunt Harriet, the woman who'd raised her and I'd known much of my life, a long letter telling her how much I loved and would miss Tracy. I was too cowardly to call.

The cards rained down on the table. Zoe had her back to me, and her stance stiffened.

Michael set down the rest of the bags and came over to the couch. He sat beside me. "Everyone knows you were in a horrible accident, and it's a miracle you're alive. That's what you need to remember."

He scratched Anne's neck. "We're all very grateful for that."

I couldn't make myself look at him and went on as if he hadn't said anything, "Do they know that I've been arrested?"

Instantly, all the air felt sucked from the room.

Zoe snorted. "No, Mom. This family is getting pretty good at hiding its dirty little secrets."

Chapter Twenty-Four

A Merry Heart

I'd never thought I'd be thankful for being physically weak and exhausted, but it allowed me to sleep. Sort of. I spent a lot of time with the TV on an old movie channel and drifted in and out of a light doze. Deep sleep brought nightmares.

In a particularly rough one, Tracy and I swilled cocktails on a beach, laughing, having a good time. Then in the odd way of dreams, Zoe and I sped off in a shiny red convertible, it's top down. I had to navigate around the skull and rib bones of a long-horned steer poking out of the blazing sand. Vultures circled overhead. I looked in the rearview mirror.

Behind us, Tracy frantically tried to corral a brood of young chicks in the small sliver of shadow thrown by a saguaro cactus. She'd grab one and shove it to safety, while another darted off into the burning desert. The red-haired barista picked up a couple of the little, yellow fluff-balls and set them swimming in a large martini glass full of purple liquid.

Tracy was too busy chasing the other chicks to notice I'd left.

"What are you doing, Mom? Those kids won't survive out here. Neither will she." Dream Zoe's eyes slashed me like daggers as she berated me in her overly-emotional teenaged way. "Tracy would make a much better mother than you!"

Circling slowly up to consciousness, I lay in bed knowing it was true. Tracy had dozens of young dancers who loved and needed her. What did my kids have but a felon for a mother?

The thought of falling asleep again scared me. Tiptoeing from the bedroom and trying not to wake Michael, I went downstairs to my nest on the couch. An "I Love Lucy" marathon played on TV. The sound was on low when Christopher came in from work a little after midnight. He kicked off his shoes and plopped into the chair beside the couch. The smell of Italian food clung to him like marinara cologne.

"Trouble sleeping, huh." It wasn't a question.

"Yeah. It's easier during the day."

He grabbed an open bag of Cheetos and started munching. "I love this one."

The episode showed Lucy visiting Rome and landing a chance to audition for a movie entitled *Bitter Grapes*. Assuming the film is about wine and hoping to prepare for an audition, she goes to an old-fashioned winery with the idea of soaking up some local color. She lands a job stomping grapes.

"Me, too." I reached over and grabbed a handful of puffs. "This and the one where she and Ethel work at the candy factory are my favorites."

We ate and watched the show. Soon, despite myself, I cracked a smile. No matter how many times I'd seen an episode of Lucy, she made me laugh.

"Reminds me of work tonight," Christopher said. "These two people wanted white wine. I asked if they'd like a Pinot Grigio or a chardonnay. The first said, 'I'll have the Pinot.' The second said, 'Me, too. Make sure the glass is clean.'

When I came back to the table with the two drinks, I said, 'Here are your two Pinot Grigios. Which one wanted the clean glass?'"

He'd said it with such a straight face I fell for it. Such a corny joke I couldn't help laughing.

"Then this guy came in and asked if we cooked vegan. I told him no. They are too stringy and hard to slice."

I snorted out-loud and had to put my hand over my mouth to keep from waking Michael and Zoe. The jokes just rolled out of him, one after another, like a stand-up comic. Christopher had been funny since he learned about knock-knock jokes when he was a preschooler and started making up his own. I'd never appreciated his sense of humor quite so much.

It felt great to laugh.

Then I got a fit of the giggles like I did in church as a little girl when I was supposed to be quiet while Papa preached. The more I tried to stifle them and keep quiet the worse it got. Christopher laughed with me.

At the same time, Lucy began high prancing steps around the vat of grapes. Acting like she knew what she was doing, she tried to outdo the other worker who got angry. The other lady slipped and fell, then pelted grapes at Lucy. Soon they were rolling around in the grapes like mud wrestlers, covered with purple goo.

Lucy had certainly soaked up lots of color. I nearly busted a gut.

I clamped my teeth tight trying to be quiet. My belly convulsed in and out, hurting the ribs bruised by the seat belt. I wrapped my arms around myself, rocking. Tears came to my eyes.

By the time they gushed over, I was sobbing. Crying hard. It took Christopher only a beat to realize my emotions had flipped. He scooted over beside me and hugged me to him, cradling my head against his chest as if I were the child.

"It's okay, Mom. It'll be okay."

His deep man's voice rumbled under my head. When had my baby gotten so large? He wasn't as filled out as Michael yet, but he was a couple inches taller and well on his way.

"You're just stressed and still recovering. Have you prayed?"

How could I admit to my son that even before the awful thing I'd done I felt like God was deaf to my pleas. I'd never felt so separated from him. I murmured something indistinct. Christopher held me, and we sat that way for a minute while I got control of myself.

"You always tell Zo and me that we can draw fearlessly, and confidently, and boldly to the throne of grace to find help in good time for *every* need."

I sniffed back the last of my tears and managed to straighten up. Christopher's face looked blurry through my wet eyes.

"I'd say we've got a few needs right now," he said.

"When'd you become so wise?" I asked, swiping my face with my fingers.

He handed me a tissue. "How about I pray?"

We held hands and my precious son, this young man

who I loved more than my own life, prayed simply and honestly from his heart. He thanked God for saving my life, asked him to heal me, comfort our family and Tracy's, give his dad wisdom at work, and lead Zoe to make the right decisions.

For the first time in weeks, God's peace enveloped me.

Chapter Twenty-Five

Let Us Not Neglect
Our Meeting Together

Despite Christopher's efforts the night before, depression greeted me like an old friend the next morning. Numbness had come to feel good. Hiding from the world felt safe, and I didn't care if I ever left the house again.

Heck, I never wanted to leave my bed again.

Michael wouldn't have it. "It's Sunday, Sheena. You need to go to church."

I groaned and plopped the pillow over my face.

"Your church family loves and cares about you. I've fielded non-stop calls, texts, and emails. They want to see for themselves that you are recovering. That you're all right."

I'd been ignoring every text and email. The undeserved kindness left me emotionally drained and I didn't know how to answer.

"I'm not all right." The words came out muffled.

Michael yanked the pillow off and sat down beside me. The edge of the bed sagged under his weight causing me to roll against him. I tried to pull back, but it was a losing proposition. I laid curled around his solid form knowing trying to resist him would be useless, too.

His tone was patient, but I knew him well enough to recognize police-chief-stern under the public-servant-soft tone of his words. "You need to set an example for your daughter. Zoe's been hiding in her room for a couple weeks."

Michael brushed a strand of hair out of my eyes. "Besides, it will do you good."

"People will talk," I mumbled into his hip.

"Of course, they'll talk. It's what people do." His thumb caressed my satin clad arm. "You've got to face the music some time. What better place to start than church? At least, there we're certain you *do* have supporters."

I'd made Kara show me the copies of the Graitney Gazette from the days after the car wreck. The accident, Tracy's death, and my recovery had been headline news for over a week. Eric, Kara's husband, knew from his law enforcement contacts that I'd been arrested and my blood work had been sent to the state crime lab.

In the initial coverage, he'd kept the printed version of

the truth to a casual, "The accident appears to be weather-related. An official cause has yet to be determined."

"He didn't print that I'd been arrested?" I asked her when she came to visit after I'd gotten home.

A militant look lit her eyes. "It could be years before they convene a grand jury and that's only *if* your blood alcohol content is .08, which it won't be." She'd never doubted me for a moment. "Sheena, I know you. You would never drive drunk."

Wish I shared her conviction.

Dallas and Fort Worth are such large cities and accidents, sadly, so common, my wreck earned only a single sentence on their media outlets. Still, I knew how things worked in a small town. Rumors were flying.

"Come on." Michael stood. "You've got an hour. I'm going to go wake Zoe. We're going to church as a family."

He paused in the doorway. All traces of cop were gone. His face registered only the love and concern of a good husband. "Besides, Sheena, no matter what it looks like to you, we have a lot to be thankful for. We might have attended two funerals last week instead of one."

He'd been patient with me, but I knew having to deal with work issues and concern over Zoe had been stressful for him. I'd managed to make his burden incalculably worse.

Michael turned and I watched him walk away down

the long hallway.

After being there for me, I owed it to him to face the world. Well, at least the church. I don't know what he said to get Zoe out of her room, but an hour later, we all piled into his Jeep Cherokee.

Zoe and I are alike in so many ways. We both prefer to wear bright colors, and we rarely leave the house without our faces on. That morning I noticed my daughter, like me, had carefully fixed her hair. She'd used the straightener until each strand shone like the polished black walnut of our dining room table, her make-up expertly applied.

Our masks were in place. Yet, we both wore plain, dark-colored slacks and tops, as if hoping to blend in and disappear. Even the flashy jewelry we preferred was absent.

"We look like we're going to a funeral," I quipped, closing the car door.

Immediately, I realized what I said. "Sorry. Sorry guys…I didn't mean to…." I lapsed into silence, images of Tracy racing through my mind.

One of the kids gasped and I could feel Michael stiffen. He reached over and turned the radio on, finding a Christian music station. I berated myself and questioned the wisdom of leaving the house the entire drive to church.

I hadn't been out in public or even been around anyone yet. The family had used the excuse of my weakened condition to keep people away from the hospital and house. Kara was the only friend I'd seen. My hallucination of Tracy visiting me at the hospital, although a painfully sweet memory, didn't count. It was just an illusion.

What if people shunned me? Or worse yet yelled at me for killing Tracy? Sometimes I felt my family wanted to. I couldn't bear seeing my friends' disappointed, angry faces. Going to church had been a stupid decision. I needed to go home. I had to go home.

Too late.

Michael pulled into the lot, nosing into an empty space. I turned to beg him to pull back out again, but he turned off the vehicle, hopped out, and hurried around the car to open my door. The sight of our red brick church, white trim surrounding the large stain-glass windows, and tall steeple calmed me a little. Michael was right. Church had always been a safe place for me. If I had to be tossed to the lions, at least it was there.

Michael helped me out of the car and gave me his arm. I appreciated the courtly gesture. The physical weakness was real, and the large dressing on my thigh made walking awkward, even in wide-legged pants. It seemed hard to believe that a few weeks ago I ran four miles a day and thought about joining the new yoga studio.

We'd barely reached the sidewalk before I heard an excited yelp and Gabby, the NEST leader, came running with long, athletic strides from a car parked nearby. "Sheena! You look great! God is so good!"

She threw her arms around me and pulled me into a welcoming hug. Over her shoulder, I saw the people streaming through the front doors freeze and look our direction. My insides knotted. Suddenly, Dolores and Kara rushed back down the steps, along with other friends. The huddle of people around me grew. They passed me from arm to arm as folks embraced me and wiped away tears, telling me how they'd spent all night in prayer for me the evening of the accident.

The outpouring of love was so unexpected, so foreign to what had been going on in my mind, that elation rose inside me like a soap bubble floating upward in the sunshine. Iridescent. Weightless. Free.

Yet at the same time, it felt just as insubstantial. Delicate. Fragile. Ready to pop.

They didn't know the truth. If they did, they wouldn't be acting this way. I didn't deserve all this love. I was a phony. A fraud. Not a good person at all. Deep shame filled me, as surely as if I'd kicked a puppy.

After a few minutes, Michael managed to swoop the whole family through the throng of well-wishers and into the sanctuary. Everyone treated Zoe normally, and I was more grateful for that than for anything else. The thought of people shunning her was unbearable.

Christopher had told me that rumors had gotten out about a pornographer scamming local kids, but no names had leaked so far. Neither, it seemed, had Zoe's pictures. Not yet. Michael said that was because the sextortionists did their sick trading on the dark web where normal people don't go. I prayed everything stayed there.

We slid into our usual pew. From the other side of the room, Cecilia watched me without a smile. She quickly averted her eyes, then leaned over and whispered something to her husband. A stickler for following the rules, she was one of the strictest mothers I knew. We'd known each other a long time. Even though we weren't close, I considered her a friend, and her intense whispering about me hurt.

Ida leaned forward as she chatted with another one of Graitney's prominent families sitting in front of her. Her twin daughters sat beside her, listening eagerly. They all glanced toward me, saw me watching, and hurriedly gazed away.

I quit looking around the sanctuary and stared at the announcement bulletin, not seeing a word. Finally, the music started.

Michael, as usual, knew what was best. During the service, the crushing burden I'd been feeling lightened. I prayed hard for Tracy's Aunt Harriet. I couldn't get the anguish she had to be going through out of my mind.

However, for the first time since I'd found out about Tracy, my spirit quit hurting for her. As a believer, despite dying so young, she was at peace.

Even knowing that, for the last week, my thoughts had continually dwelt on all of Tracy's dreams and plans. She loved kids and they adored her, as evidenced by her dance studio's popularity.

I couldn't rid myself of the memory of her confiding to me that now that she was divorced she wanted to foster-parent an older child, with the end goal of adopting. With the bright pink tips in her hair and tiny build, she'd looked hardly older than a teen herself, but her huge brown eyes had burned with excitement. Her marriage had been so miserable that it had been a long time since I'd seen her that passionate about anything but dance. That happy for the future.

Not only had I cut short her life, but I'd deprived a needy child of a loving mother. It was one of many thoughts that consumed me. Sadly, it was also one of the only things I remembered until coming to in the hospital. At least, I assumed that had happened that evening. Fears of what filled the empty time-gap took their toll on my mind.

However, as I sang worship songs and let Pastor Mike's words wash over me – I still couldn't concentrate – my agitated soul experienced an hour of much needed rest.

I hoped to escape the moment the service ended, but Michael had other plans. He led the family to the annex for coffee hour. Gabby, Kara, and Mati, another friend from Bible study, found me a chair and made a phalanx around me. They kept the crush of people away, allowing only one or a two at a time to come up and talk to me.

Even so, friends' well-meaning words ran together. My fuzzy brain struggled to process it all.

"I sent out an emergency prayer request on social media the moment I heard you'd been CareFlited. Friends around the world were praying."

"The Lord didn't let me sleep. I spent all night on my knees."

"When Gabby called me to pray and said they didn't expect you to make it, I knew everything was in God's perfect timing, but I couldn't understand how he could take you from us at such a young age. Thankfully, he didn't."

"I've never met you, Mrs. McKenzie. We just moved to town a couple of weeks ago. Our realtor told us what had happened, and my entire church back home in Kansas has been praying for you and the other people involved in the accident."

"Such a tragedy about poor Miss Tracy. Heartbreaking. But the good Lord knew your family still needs you here."

That last, said by elderly Mr. Yates, cut through the

fog. Didn't many more people still need Tracy to be here
than needed me?

"Thank you," I said to him, then motioned to Kara.
"Could you find Michael, please? I want to go home."

The moment we walked into the kitchen, I gripped the
edge of the table and fell onto the chair, unable to make it
to the couch before collapsing.

"Are you okay, Mom?" Christopher asked with a
furrowed forehead.

"Just exhausted, hon. That took a lot out of me."

Zoe called from where she stood with the refrigerator
open. "I'll make lunch."

Laughter bubbled out of her, a sound I'd wondered if
I'd ever hear again. It made my momma's heart soar.

"Let me rephrase," she said, "I'll heat up some
leftovers. We have tons."

Michael stood behind me, his large hands massaging
my shoulders. "Church wasn't so bad, was it?"

"People were whispering about me."

His hands paused. "If they were, you weathered it just
fine. Didn't she kids?"

Both kids nodded and agreed, as if they'd talked about
supporting me.

"You were a rock star, Mom." Christopher filled a
glass with ice, then tea, and handed it to me. He started
filling others for the rest of the family.

Michael gave my shoulders an extra squeeze. His breath tickled my ears as he leaned down and whispered, "Talk to Zoe."

I patted his hand where it lay on my shoulder. It *was* time for everything to stop revolving around me. Zoe had to get out there and face her demons, too. I looked at the large, color-coded calendar on the wall.

"Looks like tomorrow you've got a choreography session with the Kickers scheduled, Zo."

She paused, a pan of lasagna in hand. "Do I have to go?" Her gaze flicked back and forth between me and her dad.

Setting the casserole down, she buried her head in the fridge, pulling out other leftovers, piling them on the counter. I completely understood her not wanting to expose herself to whatever rumors were out there, but she couldn't hide forever either.

Michael crossed to the cupboard and removed a stack of dishes, saying casually, but in a no nonsense tone, "You took on an obligation when you accepted the position of an officer." He set a plate down for each of us. "We McKenzies fulfill our duties."

"The excuse of my accident has run its course," I added, hoping I sounded sincere. "Look at me, up and about now and everything."

She sent me a commiserating grin. We shared a

moment as kindred spirits.

"Watch this, sis." Christopher put one finger on top of his head, arm bent ballerina style. "I could take your place with all those hot girls, if you want."

He twirled, his long leg and big foot whacked the plant stand full of orchids which stood in the bay window.

Whooping, he caught the wobbly stand before anything crashed to the tile floor. "See, I've got some moves I could show them."

Zoe giggled. "You'd better save those awesome dance skills for the talent show, bro." Her gaze met mine. "You're right. I'm a big girl. It's time I started acting like it."

We ate a pleasant lunch, and I took a lovely, dreamless nap afterward. It felt for a brief time, like life might get back to normal.

Chapter Twenty-Six

Bistro Banter

On his way to work the next morning, Michael dropped Zoe at the school dance room where Miss Williams and the girls were working. Zoe had looked grim but determined when she left the house. I felt the familiar flutter of worry, but I was still too overwhelmed by all we already faced to even go there. I couldn't handle one more thing. I'd been trying to remind myself to take every thought captive and trust God. Even though he and I hadn't exactly been close lately.

Kara called, asking me to lunch at a new bistro in town. "You need to get out of the house, Sheena. It's not good for you to stay cooped up," she said when I declined.

"I did get out. I went to church. It exhausted me."

"We've got early reservations. It won't be too busy

yet." She sounded determined. "I'll drop you at the door, and when we are done, I'll come back and pick you up. Super simple."

It would have been nice to stay hidden, and I wanted to, even though home felt like a prison at times, too. A little foretaste of the future, perhaps?

She and Michael were right. I needed to get out, even if just to set an example for Zoe. For the second time in as many days, I dolled myself up. A peacock blue shirt over a long white skirt hid the bandage. The gash in my leg had been so jagged normal stitches weren't enough because I'd lost skin, too. Hence, the awkward dressing. I slid on some cute wedge sandals which were easy to walk in.

Kara gave a low whistle when I got into her car. "You look great. Not to be mean or anything, but you looked bad for a while there. Now look at you. Pretty, but so skinny."

"I haven't fit into this skirt in five years." I shook my head. "There are better ways to drop the weight."

She smirked. "No kidding. We all hope you don't try this last escapade again. You have no idea what you put us all though."

A surge of emotion welled through me. The sense of God's protection and provision for my life battled constantly with shame and grief. The slightest thing could trigger it. I bit my lip determined not to cry. We were going to have an ordinary, enjoyable lunch.

While she drove, Kara talked about her daughter who just graduated high school but didn't know what to do with her life.

"We've encouraged her to go to college, of course, but she can't figure out a major. Eric's gotten desperate and even suggested journalism. As if that's a stable career nowadays." She barked a short derisive laugh.

Talking about her problems gave me the opportunity to pull myself together. Kara dropped me off in front of the new restaurant, and I headed inside. The place was cute, decorated like a French cafe. Stone walls, painted to look old, held pots of trailing ivy. White cast iron tables and chairs with Toile-covered cushions dotted the room and the outdoor garden area.

The host seated us in a back corner of the patio, and we perused the menu of brunch items, soups, salads, and sandwiches. The tall walls of the surrounding buildings kept the courtyard shaded enough that even in the Texas summer it felt pleasant. Large potted trees and shrubs gave each table a sense of privacy.

The server had just taken our order when I heard a familiar voice.

"I think something is being hushed up because her husband is the chief of police," came the bossy twang of Kuddles Malik.

Kara put down the water glass she'd been holding, her

eyes wide. I put a finger to my lips and surreptitiously looked about. Around the corner, nearly hidden by a huge flowering oleander bush, I spotted the platinum spiked hair of Kuddles. Aimée Alterman's honey tousled locks were on the opposite side of the table, Jenifer Duran's long, multi-bleached hair visible beside her. The Blondes. A server delivered a round of mimosas and picked up a lot of empty champagne flutes.

"Looks like they've been here since brunch," Kara hissed. "I wonder how many of those they've gone through."

I caught her eye and jerked my head to the side. She caught on. We quietly stood, lifted our table, and moved it about six inches, far enough for the bush and the edge of the wall to hide us. We could still hear just fine. Of course, the fact that The Blondes were three-quarters smashed didn't hurt. Their voices were rather loud, and they probably assumed they were the only people seated outside.

"What do you think really happened, Kuddles?" asked Aimée's clipped, nasal voice.

"Maybe she was texting while driving? In a fight with that friend of hers? Speeding? High? Who knows. I was talking to an acquaintance who is a policewoman and usually quite chatty." She paused as if for dramatic effect. "Not a word. I couldn't get a word out of her about what really happened. I bet they've all been told to keep quiet. I'm sure there's more to the story than we've heard."

The voice of Jennifer Duran, who spoke with a slight Latino accent, drifted over to us, "We don't know Sheena did anything wrong. It could all be just what it appears to be, a tragic accident."

Aimée and Kuddles joined in cruel laughter.

Kuddles said dismissively, "You're so naive."

Even though I couldn't see her, I knew poor Jennifer was blushing. She often seemed uncomfortable around the other two.

"Get real, Jen," Aimée added, as always on Kuddles' side. "Cars don't just hit another car and flip over and over like that for nothing."

"It'd been raining," Jennifer's soft voice insisted.

"How can she stand being a Blonde?" I whispered to Kara.

"Whatever happened," Kuddles' bossy voice went on, "that woman's a bad influence. She should *not* be around our girls."

"They shouldn't go over to the McKenzie house, at least," Aimée agreed.

I started to rise out of my chair, nails biting into my balled fists. Kara clamped a hand on my arm and pulled me back down.

"Her daughter seems okay," Kuddles said in a tone that

sounded as if she were granting Zoe pardon for being born near a strip mall instead of a fashion mall. Their version of the wrong side of the tracks.

"Besides, our girls like the child," Aimée added.

"Well, I'm removing Sheena McKenzie from all volunteer duties," Kuddles said. That settled things. "We can at least keep the mother from having anything to do with the Kickers."

Good thing Kara held me down. Suddenly, all those tasks I'd been assigned and didn't want to do seemed the most important things in the world to accomplish.

I could hear Michael telling Zoe, "We McKenzies fulfill our duties."

"What are you doing this afternoon?" I asked sotto voce.

She raised her palms and shrugged. No plans.

"Let's get at it," I said softly. "I want to knock off all my Kicker mom duties before that bi...Blonde can do anything about it."

Kara looked nervous but agreed. Thankfully, after the latest round of mimosas, the Blondes left without ever realizing we were so close by.

I calmed down, making myself talk about pleasant, normal things while we ate a delicious lunch of French onion soup and croissant sandwiches. Then we tackled my list.

It's amazing what sympathy will do to open doors and get people to agree to things they might not ordinarily have wanted to do. Sympathy or curiosity. I ran down every person on my list. No one refused to see me. All mouthed concern and said kind things, but curious eyes and the occasional bold question let me know my instinct had been correct. I'd been a story for the last couple of weeks, and people wanted to see for themselves how I was doing. How I looked.

If I acted guilty.

The anger scorching through my veins like heat lightning at the thought of tipsy Blondes casting aspersions on me, kept me focused as I knocked off every name assigned to me. Ridiculous because as far as I knew, they could have been right and I *had* been drunk driving.

They might have a speck in their eyes, but I certainly had a log in my own.

It was nearly suppertime when Kara dropped me back at home. Michael met me at the door.

"Where have you been?" He glowered down at me. "I've been calling."

Chapter Twenty-Seven

Heart To Heart

I reached in my purse and pulled out my phone. Six calls and ten texts from Michael. "I'm sorry, honey. I've had it off while Kara and I ate lunch, and I forgot to turn it back on."

"While you did what?" he asked, his calm tone belied by short and snappy words. "You can't just disappear. Not after what happened."

"I'm sorry." I slid past him and dropped onto a chair. "Kara and I rounded up Kicker parents to volunteer for summer camp duties, football games, and people to buy ads in the programs."

"You had to do that today? Without telling me?" He loomed over me. His square jaw gritted tight.

"I'm way behind." A weak excuse.

His eyes were slits. His shoulders bunched. Heat seemed to come off him in waves. Michael never got mad at me – ever.

His hand flung out and I flinched. He'd never touched me except in love, but I wasn't used to him being upset either.

"Look at you," he said, the hand pointing, not hitting. "You look like you've been pulled behind a pickup truck down a dirt road. Damn it, Sheena. We just got you well enough to stand up."

His arm dropped and he kneeled, grabbing my hand. Crouching beside me, our eyes level, his anger visibly drained away.

"She-Girl," his voice shook. "I don't think you have any idea how badly you scared me. Scared all of us. We almost lost you. It was touch and go for days there. We didn't know if you'd make it. Then when you're finally well enough to be on your feet just long enough to go to church you...you disappear? All day!"

Seeing Michael so upset, the man always cool and collected no matter what chaos swirled around him, rocked me. Guilt trooped back in. I felt awful and had no excuse. I could hardly tell him I got my panties in a wad over what some mean moms said about me.

Holding his hand against my cheek, I said, "I'm sorry, honey. I wasn't thinking. I thought you'd be proud of me for getting out of the house, but I didn't think about you worrying. It won't happen again. I'll let you know when I'm going out."

His eyes closed for a moment as if in prayer.

"Thanks." He let out a pent-up breath. "It's not forever. Just until you're a hundred percent. I *need* to know you're okay. I can't do what I have to do if I'm worried about you."

My heart twisted with familiar guilt. What did I do to deserve such a great husband?

My anger at the Blondes had driven me all afternoon, but I felt as wiped out as a soggy dish rag. Even though remorse and appreciation still battled for prominence when I thought of the nice things people had done for our family, I was happy to have a frozen casserole to pop in the oven. Then I laid down on the couch without the energy to even turn on the TV. Michael had run back up to work.

I woke to the sound of arguing in the kitchen. Zoe and Emily. When had they come home? They probably didn't know I was in the other room.

"How can you stand them?" Emily's voice sounded sharp and frustrated.

"You were just as happy to be a Kicker officer as me."

"I *am* glad to be an officer, but that doesn't mean The Greats have to be our new best friends. You don't have to hang around them all the time, you know. You aren't even the same person anymore."

"What's that mean?" Zoe's voice took on a harsh tone.

"You laughed with them today when Layla said that if that rumor about local kids is true, there might be kids at our school who are now porn stars."

I strained my ears, but Zoe stayed silent.

Emily went on, "Those girls probably think having nude pictures on the Internet is cool."

"They don't think that!"

Emily's voice rose defensively. "I guess you'd know. Seeing as how you're their new BFF. You *never* would have laughed at something like that before."

She had no idea what Zoe had been going through lately.

"Even if they do think so, thinking it's *cool* is better than other things people could be thinking or saying," Zoe answered, hurt layered thick beneath the sarcastic tone.

It didn't seem Emily noticed.

"Like what?" Emily paused before spitting out, "Like it's *sick* and *disgusting*, which it totally is. Sick and disgusting to have naked pictures out there for any yucky old man to lust over."

Now, Zoe's voice grew angry. "Right, sick and

disgusting. How would you like to be one of those kids and be called disgusting? Those poor kids that the pervs got pictures of are *victims*, Emily. They... are... the... *victims*, you idiot!"

Both Emily and I sucked in breath at the same time.

"So, *I'm* the idiot?"

I waited to hear Zoe say, "Yeah," and Emily to reply, "Yeah?" "Yeah!" "Yeah!" Like they would have as children and get into a name-calling fight, which would have cleared the air.

Instead, Emily voice shaking said, "Good to know how you really feel."

Someone clomped across the kitchen and the back-door slammed shut. I quickly lay back and closed my eyes. A moment later, I felt Zoe standing over me.

"You're awful at faking sleep, Mom."

Pushing my hair out of my face, I sat up. "Sorry, sweetie. I didn't mean to eavesdrop."

Zoe sat down and scooted over beside me.

I slid an arm around her. "Oh, sweetie. I'm so sorry. I'm sure you and Emily will make up."

She shrugged, but didn't say anything.

I couldn't help asking, "Do The Greats have any idea that one of the people they are talking about is you?"

"No. I don't think so." Zoe shook her head.

"I gather you're hoping if they do find out it's you they

will think it's cool."

She looked like she had as a child when I'd caught her sneaking quarters out of my purse for the neighborhood ice cream truck. "Is it bad if I do?"

I thought a moment. "You told Emily that the kids this happened to are victims."

Her little body deflated. "Dad and I've talked about it a lot, and I get it now. I was used. All those kids on that computer were used. Sickos like that man are good at manipulating young people. It's what they do."

She fiddled with threads in an artfully placed hole in her jean shorts. "But if people at school find out one of them is me, I'd rather The Greats think I was sending sexy pictures to a boyfriend."

"Like you believed you were doing?"

"Yeah, like I believed I was doing."

We sat there a moment, each lost in our own thoughts.

"Zo, why did you send those pictures? Did you want to have sex with…Drew?"

It was hard to even say the name of the innocent boy she'd thought she was talking to. Thoughts of the man behind it all, who might be her dad's age or older, still made me sick.

"No. Eew! That's gross." Her fingers tore at the hole, making it bigger. "I just wanted a boyfriend like the other girls."

I understood the teenaged desperation to be part of the cool group.

"Do those girls –" I started to ask, but she quickly cut me off.

"No, idea. I mean it's not like we talk about stuff like that. But when Drew…I mean whoever it was… asked for some pictures, I thought maybe it *is* what you do with a boyfriend. How would I know?"

I laced my fingers through the hand that wasn't tearing up her shorts. "Daddy and I have talked to you about this. We thought you understood that you don't have to sleep with boys to get them to like you. The right man will wait until you're married."

She didn't look at me, but her hand squeezed mine.

"I *know* that. We've talked about it in youth group, too." Zoe blew out a puff of air that sent wisps of her layered bangs flying. "But it was pictures, not fornicating like the Bible prohibits. Still, I knew…I *did* know it was the wrong thing, but it felt okay, somehow, too." She seemed to struggle to find a way to help me understand. "The Greats all have boyfriends. They parade them around the halls at school and at every game. Suddenly, I was one of The Greats and at their houses…, but I still felt like the awkward little sister when they went off with their boyfriends."

She was the youngest in that group, something that had

worried me.

"Then one night there were a bunch of kids from different schools who'd come to hang out. I met Drew and we clicked. It was so awesome to feel grown up and wanted, like the other girls. I didn't know it was a one-time thing. When I got the message from him the next day, I felt like I was walking on sunbeams."

"But the other girls didn't know about him?"

"I kind of dropped hints that I was seeing someone. A guy who liked me." A shy smile played across her beautiful face. "They loved my secret romance and enjoyed trying to get details out of me."

Zoe paused and twisted toward me so I could see her. "I liked the attention. The guy I *thought* was Drew said that pretty soon we were going to tell everyone we were together. Then I was going to be just like the other girls with a really awesome boyfriend. He's cute, and popular. A football player.

"For the moment, I had something even The Greats didn't have: a secret romance." Her face was intense, willing me to understand. "I played up the part about him being from a larger town. A sport star with a long-time girlfriend. His girlfriend's mom is sick so he couldn't just dump her. He's too good a guy for that. They are going off to different colleges in the fall. So obviously, they'd break up then, and he could be with me. The Greats ate it up.

They loved the whole mysterious lover idea. Thought I was some kind of femme fatale."

That's what I got for letting her watch so many old movies.

"Tell me I haven't ruined my life forever. You had boyfriends before you met Daddy, right?"

I could hear hope in her voice.

"You're right. I bloomed late, so I was naive and didn't always have the best taste in the guys I dated. Then I met your dad and fell super hard for him. You know, that whole older man in a uniform thing. I'm just fortunate he's such a good guy."

Anne jumped up on my lap, and I lifted her up to my face and gave her a snuggle. It was time to get the limelight off me. The last thing I wanted Zoe doing was following in my not-so-stellar footsteps.

"The point is no matter how bad this looks right now your life can turn out just fine. Your dad and I love you, no matter what. I want you to remember that."

I set Anne back down, and she curled into a donut and made herself comfortable on my lap.

Zoe rubbed the cat's head. "I know. I couldn't survive all this without you."

I swallowed hard, managing to say, "Your dad is as determined as they come. I wouldn't be surprised if he cracked this case himself."

"Dad's already checked into the real Drew. The sicko stayed pretty close to the truth, in case I checked Drew out on other social media sites. He does play football. His team is busy with two-a-day practices. There wasn't much chance of my running in to him this summer. What would have happened if I had? How embarrassing!"

"But the photographs?" I couldn't help myself. It was so unlike her. "How did you jump to those?"

"It wasn't right away. By then I'd fallen for him. We already had a future planned out. Drew...," she shuddered, "I mean, that guy, told me it's what you do in adult relationships. I didn't want to be a kid any more. I wanted to be an adult. So, I had to do adult things, right?"

I stifled a sigh.

"Besides, he missed me. He said I'm so gorgeous that just the thought of our private pictures got him through the day." She stared into the distance, then seemed to steel herself to go on. "We surfed websites of 1940s and 50s pinup girls, like Marilyn Monroe to get ideas for poses. Did you know she was a Playboy centerfold?" Her voice rose in pitch a bit defensively. "Somehow seeing how artsy the photos are, with big-name movie stars and all, made it seem okay. I mean, you can buy those pictures on eBay."

My skin crawled, but I remained silent as she processed all this. It was the first time we'd really talked about it.

"What do you think now?"

She choked out a laugh that wasn't a happy sound. "First, I've got to make sure I'm in a relationship with who I think I am."

"And...?"

"And if those *stupid* pictures never show up, I'll be eternally grateful. All I think about is that there could be hundreds of sick old men staring at what I should have saved for my husband. I realize now why the way you and Daddy raised me is the right way. I used to think it was just old-fashioned and, frankly, kinda dumb." Her shoulders started shaking.

I pulled her head against me.

"I've ruined my life."

"No, you haven't, sweetie. It's what you do now that counts. And remember, nothing's too big for God to handle."

I believed that. I really did, but the words of Mark 9:24 ran through my head: "Lord, I believe; help my unbelief!"

"That's just it, Mom. I always thought I was a good Christian. But I'm really a hypocrite. An awful fake, phony, hypocrite."

"I feel like that, too, sweetie. I always thought this kind of thing happens to other people, not good people like us...like me. But the thing is: we are 'the good Christians.' How nuts is that? Even good Christians screw up. We just screwed up."

"Big time."

"Yeah, big time."

We shared sad looks.

"I guess just being saved doesn't sanitize us, does it?" Zoe asked.

"No, it doesn't. But you do know God doesn't just forgive you of your sins before you're saved," I looked deep into Zoe's eyes, "right? He still forgives us."

"Do you feel forgiven, Mom?"

She had me there. "I'm working on it. How about you?"

Zoe shook her head. "No, I don't think God's forgiven me, at all."

I put my hand against her silky hair. "Oh, sweetie. I'm so sorry."

True, but I didn't feel particularly forgiven either.

After our talk and dinner, I took a shower and put on my jammies, feeling little better than dead when my phone chirped. I wouldn't have picked it up, except Michael was back at work, and I didn't want to worry him again. The moment I saw the name on the screen, "Kimberly Malik" it felt like I'd downed a gallon of 5-Hour Energy drinks.

I answered with my fakest Texas drawl, "Kimberly, just the woman I've been wanting to talk to."

The dead air on the other end thrilled me. Kuddles stunned silent might have been a first.

"I wanted to tell you that I've signed up all the volunteers on my list. I've checked with everyone on my donor list, too, and they all have upped their contributions from last year," I went on in a super cheery voice. "In fact, I've been informed that the donation from Nelly's Beauty Supply is the largest in Kicker history."

"I thought you were...I didn't know you were up and abo...that's a.... marvelous," she finally got out.

"I thought I'd bring kale salad to our meeting Wednesday night."

She managed to get a little of her normal bossy tone back when she said, "Don't worry about that, dear. We've got the food covered. We didn't think you'd be up to attending."

"Wouldn't miss it for the world."

Chapter Twenty-Eight

Nest News

Instead of one step forward and two steps back, the next day I felt as if I'd fallen a mile behind. I didn't admit it to Michael, but he was right. I'd pushed myself too hard. Not only was I physically exhausted, but the mental fog returned with a vengeance. My family told me that the first few days after the accident I said things that didn't make sense at all. Sometimes I'd sit with a blank stare as if I had no idea what was going on around me. I still found myself struggling to think of common words. That day, I couldn't concentrate enough to read, which had always been my favorite form of escape. Even watching local reporter Rex J. Fowler on mute as he covered a 4th of July parade was a challenge.

Christopher and Michael were at work, and Zoe had

gone shopping with some friends – she hadn't mentioned the fight with Emily – when the doorbell rang. I didn't want to get off the couch, but I made myself get up and open the door. I hoped it wasn't Kara because I wasn't up to discussing our daughters' problems.

Gabby Guthrie, my Bible study leader, stood on the front porch. As usual, she wore workout clothes, her hair pulled back into a long, shiny silver ponytail, her face glowed. She'd probably just finished her daily run. Like me, it was one of her favorite times to pray. Unlike me, who'd have been a melted mess in this heat, she looked like she could pose for a fitness catalogue.

"Oh, Sheena, I hope I'm not bothering you, but I've missed you and wanted to see how you are doing." She held out two drinks. "I brought Sonic Diet-Limeades."

I flashed her a grateful smile because the thought of making coffee seemed overwhelming, and something cool sounded way better on a Texas summer day.

"Come on in."

We walked into the living room. She moved some magazines and sat in an armchair. Her house always looked ready for a photoshoot for HGTV. Gabby was someone so accomplished you wanted not to like her, except she was too nice for that. She won everyone over. Our house tended to eclectic and a bit messy, but normally we kept the public areas tidy. I looked at my spot on the couch. Part of a magazine peaked out from between the cushions. Wedged between the various pillows were crumpled tissues. A throw blanket hung halfway onto the floor. Hopefully, she hadn't noticed the telltale orange Cheetos-dust on the sofa before I sat down.

Normally, I'd worried about the mess, but it was too much work.

"What's up?" I asked, opening my straw and sinking it into the lovely crushed ice.

It had been an idle question, just something you say, but for some reason Gabby looked uncomfortable when I glanced back at her. Nothing ever bothered her. She took a moment too long peeling the straw and pushing it into her drink, as if trying to think of how to say something.

She flashed me a smile that didn't light her eyes. "Everyone sends their well wishes. It was so good to see you at church. We can't wait until you are up to coming back to the NEST."

Images of whispering friends rushed through my mind, my foggy brain suddenly cleared.

"But not everyone?" I sat up straighter, ready to deflect a blow.

Gabby's tan didn't completely hide a flush. Her face was easier to read than my iPhone X's large screen.

"Something's happened. You can tell me." I didn't like what my mouth was saying. The last thing I needed was more bad news, but I already felt so low it was as if I had a masochistic need to pile on more pain.

She may have read something of my thoughts and tried to soften the blow. "Remember our discussion on how we are to 'count it all joy' when we meet various kinds of trials?"

I did know that and it made me feel worse for how poorly I was handling things. The last thing I felt was joyful.

Gabby twisted the straw while I nodded. "Well, we've run into a bit of a trial at the NEST, and I guess you should hear about it from me first...." She exhaled before continuing. "After church Sunday night, while some of us were talking, one of the Chicks suggested banning you from the Bible study."

"Banning me?"

"She's heard some ridiculous rumors and felt you might be a bad influence on the other women."

"Was it Cecili—" I started to ask.

Gabby cut me off an alarmed look in her wide eyes. "No. Cecilia rushed to your defense and said that it's when we are having trouble that we need to extend one another the most grace."

Our most seemingly Pharisaical member saying this shocked me almost as much as the news someone else wanted to kick me out. "She did?"

"Yes." Gabby's familiar smile returned. "Like we often talk about, we aren't to judge a person by what we see on the outside. God could be doing a work in their heart that the rest of us can't see."

If I'd been talking to Kara, who had a propensity to gossip, I would have tried to dig out information on what was going on with Cecilia, but Gabby kept confidences as strictly as a Catholic priest. I was so surprised by this new-found side of a fellow Chick that I nearly forgot what we were talking about – but not quite.

"Go on. Someone wants to kick me out."

She twisted the straw again. It squeaked annoyingly, but she didn't seem to notice. "I stopped that talk on the spot. The NEST is no place for rumors. All of us are there because we're desperate messes without God. We want to know and love Him more. We do that together, by loving and supporting one another."

Another name popped into my head. "Ida." I pictured her immaculately dressed form, with her perfect tan, blindingly white teeth, and orange hair.

"She's worried about her twins *L&O* not getting on the Kicker team next year," I said, knowing I'd figured it out. "Ida's determined to steer clear of anything or anyone who could hurt their chances." And her chance of getting in good with The Blondes.

Gabby shifted her eyes away, looking at, but probably

not seeing, the cluster of framed family photos covering the mantel. "Don't worry about who brought it up. It's all water under the bridge now. I just wanted you to know that the Chicks are behind you no matter what happens."

No matter what happens.

The rumors were probably about the very real possibility of my being indicted for intoxication manslaughter. Even though Gabby was one of my dearest friends, I didn't have the courage to confide in her. She would stand by me. For sure. But I was so disappointed in myself, I couldn't stand to see disappointment in me cloud her face. There would come the day I would have to face her and everyone, but I was not ready. When the time came, I knew I could count on her.

As to the other Chicks standing by me, I wasn't as sure. Maybe. Maybe not. No matter what, I didn't want to face their disappointment either. In some ways, having my church friends find out the truth about me made me sicker than anything the parents at school, even The Blondes, thought. It all circled back to being a hypocrite. Not being the person they thought I was.

The person I always thought I was.

The worst part was I couldn't remember. If I knew what I'd done that night, I could mentally prepare. Instead, I kept filling the gaping black hole with more and more horrible thoughts of what I'd done. Had I really gone overboard? Gotten roaring drunk? Worse? I snapped my attention back to Gabby who'd cocked her head looking at me with a funny expression. How long had my thoughts wandered?

"Thanks. I appreciate that," I managed, frantically trying to make my sluggish brain come up with another topic. "How's the painting going?"

Heavy clouds obscured the night sky and the poorly lit black road, wet from a recent shower. Moisture somewhere between mist and rain drops obscured the windshield between swipes of the wipers. I squinted trying to see the lines as I drove. Tracy gabbed away, telling me about a girl in beginning tap who was a real cut-up.

"I try to st-stay s-serious-s and keep control of the class-s." She kept giggling over her slurred speech, messing up each "s." She was drunk. "But S-smanatha can do a hundred impressions. Keeps the girls-s in s-stiches. S-she's really good at Chip and Mrs. Potts-s from *Beauty and the Beas-st…*"

Suddenly, her laughter muted, like a radio with its volume yanked down. A cosmic dimmer switch faded everything in front of my eyes to grey. Seconds stretched bizarrely. Heavy fatigue slammed me.

Yet, my brain raced while everything else froze.

I was going to be sick! Pass out!

On-coming lights blinded me just as bile rushed up my throat.

My mind screamed to hit the brakes and aim for the side of the road. My hands and feet didn't listen.

Tires squealed on the wet pavement. Loud and long.

Images flashed, as if backlit by strobe lights. Tracy midsentence, mouth open. Blood drained from her face. Skin papery-white. Brown eyes, huge with terror, pleading.

Impacting metal screeched. Nerve-grating and shrill. An explosion blew me backward.

The car flipped, over and over and over. Windows shattered into starry fragments. The passenger compartment crushed like a soda can.

The stench of burning rubber and hot fumes poisoned the rain-scented air rushing across my skin.

Someone yelled high and long as we tumbled.

My voice, screaming. Then nothing.

I woke up in my own bed shivering and covered in sweat. Had I remembered that horrible night? Or had my mind, frustrated with the inability to remember something so important, come up with its own version of events?

Whichever, I never wanted to have that dream again.

It was hard to tell if it was me reading too much into small things, but life at the McKenzie home felt strained. Michael continued to work crazy long hours, often missing meals. He had a permanently clenched look around his once smiling mouth. Zoe didn't mention Emily, which was weird after years of practically living at one another's homes.

Kara and I had a tear-filled discussion about their fight. She had no idea what it was really about. I couldn't let her know what had happened to Zoe. The fewer people who knew the better.

Besides last time I'd unburdened myself, it hadn't turned out so well.

"I guess it's normal for teenagers to make new friends," she said wiping her nose with a tissue, "but it breaks my heart. I thought they'd be best friends forever."

Me, too.

Instead of Emily, different girls flitted in and out with her. They were all perfectly polite to me and eager to be out of earshot and on their own, disappearing in a cloud of perfume and giggles.

Michael and I had discussed curtailing her time with The Greats after what had happened, but from what she'd told us they had nothing to do with her poor decisions. They were good girls as far as we knew. Ida still vouched for the families every chance she got, and she knew them better than we did.

Christopher seemed sensitive to the changed atmosphere around the house and spent his time at work or off with his buddies.

I needed something to occupy my time and thoughts. The shadow of leaves dappled the white oak floor where the sun filtered through the trees outside. It had been weeks since I'd been in my studio, a wonderful bright space Michael built for me over the garage. My eyes scanned the large worktable and rows of bright-colored glass in vertical shelving along one wall. Small sets of drawers held jewelry supplies. Tools lay neatly lined up within easy reach. Another counter contained cardboard for display cards and pretty, transparent jewelry bags.

It was time to do something besides dwelling on my problems. I went to work.

Doing an activity by muscle memory felt great. My brain improved every day, but it was still frustrating searching for words I'd known my whole life or losing track in simple conversations. The traumatic brain injury specialist couldn't tell me how long it would take my brain to rewire. She said to be patient, but I wished it would hurry up. I'd catch the kids rolling their eyes at one another when I'd ask them something they'd told me a short while ago or when I'd repeat myself, which I seemed to do often. I felt for people battling dementia.

At least, my mind was improving.

I remained nervous of what I might remember of the night of the accident, even though it was doubtful that part would ever come back. I tried to forget the horrible dream. Had I really driven drunk? It seemed so unlike me, but then I'd never been more upset in my life. I shoved the thoughts aside. Dwelling on them did no good, and my family needed me to get back to normal.

Making jewelry was my normal.

I picked up a cool smooth sheet of dichroic glass, admiring the deep golden-colored inner glow beneath the transparent surface. I particularly liked working with that type of glass because it displayed different colors depending on the light.

Cutting the glass, I made several sizes of rectangles, 11/2-inch ones for necklaces and some shorter ones for earrings with a loop to hang a matching tassel. Then I stacked them on the kiln shelf on top of some stained-glass pieces in shades of red which I'd previously cut.

It seemed so long ago.

A long zig-zag of high-temperature wire lay between the two layers of glass, for attaching earring wires, tassels, and necklace loops. A dot of glue held everything in place until ready to fire. I admired my work. It took a practiced eye to imagine the finished pieces. Part of the fun of this craft was the joy of discovery when I opened the kiln. I had an idea of what the jewelry would look like, but the firing process produced the final product.

The kiln would reach 1,500 degrees before being shut off and allowed to cool for eight hours. Rush the process and the fragile glass would crack. Too high a temperature and the glass would become liquid and roll off the shelf.

Even though I'd been making jewelry for years, it still amazed me that ordinary bits of colored glass going through a precise process of firing and high temperatures turned into works of art. No two batches came out the same. No two pieces were exactly alike. The result was an heirloom piece of jewelry worn and loved for generations.

I'd always believed that because God made us in his image, and he was the Creator of everything, a part of us longed to be creative. Whether we met that need through art, music, dance, cooking, writing, origami, or staying one step ahead of the bad guys didn't matter. Life was stagnant and dull if we didn't have a passionate pursuit.

After setting the kiln, I sang a jaunty little tune as I headed downstairs, feeling better about myself and life in general.

Chapter Twenty-Nine

Mad Axman

I had yet to return to weekly Bible study at the NEST. Despite Gabby's reassurances that the Chicks were behind me, I didn't want to face them with whatever rumors were circulating. Thursday night, I was too tired to go anyway. Besides I didn't think I could stand looking at the place Tracy usually sat and see it empty.

Christopher had the night off work, so we were all home for dinner for the first time in a while. I'd even cooked an old family favorite, an easy lemon pork chop recipe. The freezer contained meals people had brought, but I needed to be doing ordinary things. We ate silently, shoveling down food, eyes on our plates. Generally, we talked over one another as we rattled on about our days.

"Stop it."

I looked up at Zoe's sharp tone. She and Christopher glared at each other.

"Stop what?" he asked in a saintly voice.

"That thing you're doing. You know I hate it."

"What thing?" He stabbed a bit of pork, put it in his mouth, and pulled the fork out against his teeth. The metallic screech set my own teeth on edge.

"Quit it!" Zoe yelled.

He did it again.

Michael banged his fist on the table. "Kids, stop!"

All three of us jumped, surprised he raised his voice.

"Don't we have enough going on without you two tearing each other apart?" Michael slumped back in his chair, like a tire low on air.

The kids and I stared at him. New worry ate at my stomach.

"What's wrong, honey?"

He folded his arms across his chest before answering. "Nothing. Just some new issues at work."

The room fell quiet. I could hear the hum of the refrigerator and ice cubes clinking into the bin. We'd been married long enough that I knew there was something he wasn't saying.

"Because of me, Daddy?" Zoe's huge eyes looked hollow in her pale face.

"No," I said, certain of the answer. "Because of me."

Michael's gaze dropped to his lap. All the confirmation I needed. Just when I'd decided to get the attention back on helping Zoe, where it needed to be, everything once again returned to me.

"It doesn't look great to have the chief's wife indicted for Intoxication Manslaughter," I said.

My voice sounded calm, but my mind spun. Was Michael's job in jeopardy? If so, how could I fix this mess? I should get away. Far away. I'd never do that. I couldn't leave my kids or Michael.

I probably had no choice.

I *would* be far away – locked up in Huntsville. Intoxication Manslaughter was a felony of the second degree. I was staring at confinement in the penitentiary for two to twenty years.

Hummingbirds took turns outside the bay window, swooping into the red feeder, happy for their supper. The cheery room with bright yellow paint and orange and red accents blurred. I blinked against tears. I didn't have the right to cry, seeing as how it was all my fault.

Michael cleared his throat and looked up but not at me. "Don't even go there, Sheena." His gaze swept the kids. "There's nothing to worry about. Okay? You let me handle things on my end."

Despite his words, the next couple of weeks felt as if we lived in a horror movie with a mad axman lurking right outside the door. It seemed like any moment something horrible would happen. Yet, like in the movies, we went about our daily lives clueless to the terror about to strike.

I preferred hiding in my house to facing the world. Kind people treated me as the victim of a horrible accident, but I felt like I had a huge neon "guilty" sign over my head which they would notice at any moment. Wallowing in my grief became second nature. I'd feel lost without it. The happy confident woman I'd been before seemed more and more like a dream. The mess I'd become seemed real.

I longed to turn back time and thought of almost nothing except *if onlys*. If only I'd known what Zoe was up to. If only, I hadn't met Tracy that night. If only we hadn't gone for drinks. I kept obsessing over our mistakes feeling that if I could just do the right thing, I could control the future.

However, the sad truth was that even if I'd done everything right, my children's futures were not a formula. There was no if I did X + Y, I'd get Z. There never had been any guarantees. There weren't now. Still, things would be so much easier if only….

Emily never came around the house, but Zoe acted just as enamored of The Greats as ever. As far as Michael and

I knew, these were normal teenaged girls doing normal things. She said their parents were around when there were boys over and that only girls spent the night.

It wasn't as if I could just ask The Blondes. In fact, I'd rather do just about anything other than go to them with my questions. I was glad for Zoe's sake that they still let their girls hang out at our house. After the episode at the Bistro, I'd wondered about that.

It was difficult to know if she was behaving differently or if my vague worries were my own issues. I'd try to wait up for her when she was out in the evenings, but since the accident, I'd needed more sleep. Brains take longer to heal than bodies. The rule was Zoe had to wake me when she got home, but sometimes the next morning she told me she had, but I couldn't remember her doing so. Of course, my mind wasn't functioning normally. Better, but not normal. I wanted to believe her.

She'd learned her lesson the hard way, right?

Other things had changed. Zoe used to be a bit of a neat freak about her room, but now she said she was too busy to stay on top of it. I kept telling myself to ignore the mess, but it drove me nuts. Every few days, I'd go in and straighten up a little.

The sunlight poured through her bedroom windows making the ballerina-pink walls glow. When we moved into the house, Zoe chose the second-story room looking

out into the trees in the front yard because it felt like a
treehouse. Christopher took the other front-facing bedroom
with a better view of the driveway, so he could see when
his friends arrived. Framed posters from the New York
City Ballet covered Zoe's bedroom walls.

I waded in through the discarded clothes – typically,
she tried on at least a dozen outfits before making up her
mind each day – and threw things into the laundry basket I
carried. How could she stand to live this way? Picking up
the khaki-colored skirt she'd worn Saturday night, I caught
a whiff of something that smelled like a seedy bar.

I held it up to my nose and sniffed. The distinct scent
of beer clung to the pleated fabric. Were those kids
drinking at those houses? After all the talks Michael and
I'd had with her? And all the denials she'd made? This was
the last straw. More than a straw; this felt like the Sequoia
breaking the camel's back.

Snatching the rest of her dirty laundry, I smelled every
item like a deranged drug dog. There was the jean jacket
she'd loved and insisted I buy even though it had been too
big three years ago. Now it fit perfectly. There were lacy
camisoles. When Zoe had brought them home, proud of the
bright pink-striped bag they were in, Christopher grabbed
it and laughed, asking her if she thought she'd ever fill out
enough to be a Victoria's Secret angel. I sifted through
mounds of creamy, soft t-shirts, her favorite brand. She

owned every color.

Mostly, I detected the sweet mixture of freesia, apple blossoms and Honeysuckle that were part of the Taylor Swift perfume she loved. I'd been in enough dives during my college days to recognize the beer smell on that skirt, the only place I found it.

Marching to the laundry room, I ran over options in my mind. Asking The Blondes wouldn't do any good. After overhearing them talking about me, I couldn't very well call them up and demand to know if they allowed underage drinking in their homes. Not when they suspected me of drinking and driving. I thought of completely banning her from their houses, but it wasn't practical. Not as long as Zoe remained a Kicker officer. Maybe she shouldn't remain an officer. Michael and I had some serious things to discuss.

Everything went into the wash except the skirt, which I left lying on top of the drier. Zoe came in as I finished one of the last loads. Precisely folded stacks of her clothes lined the countertop in the laundry room. If only I could put her life back in order so easily.

I snatched up the offending skirt and waved it like a battle flag. "Explain why this smells like beer, young lady?"

Zoe shrugged casually. "I guess it's 'cause I accidentally sat in some spilled beer."

"Ah ha! There was beer there. I knew it!"

She looked at me with innocent doe eyes. "Yeah. Layla's dad was drinking it. We were hanging out by the Malik's pool. He'd been out there earlier, and when I sat down, I knocked over the can he'd left on the arm of the lounge chair."

I looked at my daughter, my mouth hanging open wide enough to catch flies. I snapped it shut. "Oh. Right."

"Can you wash it, please," she added, knowing manners went a long way with me. "I'd like to wear it this weekend."

Smiling sweetly, Zoe flounced into the kitchen, and I stood holding the evidence I'd thought proved she lied to me about what went on at those houses. I should have felt better after hearing her completely plausible explanation, but I didn't. Instead, I wondered if I'd just been had. What in the world was really going on with her? I hated being so suspicious, but I'd learned a hard truth, too. I didn't know my daughter as well as I thought I did.

Would I ever trust her completely again? Or was I letting my disillusionment with myself color my view of my child?

Thankfully, High Kicker dance camp was the next

week in Houston. Originally, I'd planned to be one of the chaperones, but since I still wasn't one hundred percent, Kara took my place. That made me feel good. I trusted her, as I did Dolores who was also one of the parents attending.

The week passed in a lovely quiet haze of work and catching up on reading.

I felt guilty, but it was a relief to have Zoe out of the house and not have to worry about her every minute she was out of sight. I pointed it out as we got ready for bed the night before she was due back.

"I almost dread having her home again. Things have been a lot calmer around here. For some reason, she and Christopher have been continually picking on each other lately. It's weird because they've always gotten along well."

"Everyone is stressed," Michael said.

I sat brushing my hair at the antique vanity, watching him in the mirror.

One of my favorite things about our house was our bedroom and sitting room which stretched across the entire back of the house, its second-story perch overlooking the backyard. My desk framed by one dormer window and the window-seat nestled in the other were perfect perches for a momma bird to keep an eye on her teenage-chicks and their friends as they splashed in the pool below.

"You can say that again." I stopped brushing, noticing

how much he'd changed recently.

The purple smudges under his eyes had faded, but new lines took their place. His face looked thinner. Michael peeled off his shirt. He'd lost weight. He was still a large man, but some of his muscle mass had shrunk. Not surprising. He often missed meals and didn't have the time to lift weights with Christopher anymore.

I looked away from the depressing sight of what the physical toll of carrying these burdens had done to him and studied my own reflection. An older version of Zoe looked back at me. A few silver strands shone brightly in my dark hair. Normally shoulder length, it had gotten longer since I hadn't been able to get to the salon. Weaving it into a loose braid, I wondered if it was time to start coloring it, adding grey hair to the list of things about my life I wanted to disguise.

Michael came up behind me and put his hand over mine before I slipped on the elastic band. He moved my hand away and combed through my hair with his fingers, letting it stream over my shoulders. Leaning down, he kissed the side of my neck.

"Leave it loose for a while."

A jolt of nervous energy surged through me. We hadn't been together since the accident. I'd been avoiding it. The intimacy would make Michael feel better. For him, sex fixed most everything. But guilt left me feeling ugly, damaged, defiled. How could he look at me the way he had before?

He tilted my head back to kiss me, and I closed my eyes, pretending nothing had changed.

Chapter Thirty

Dance Camp

The phone rang in the middle of the night. Grabbing it and punching it on, I noticed the time – 1:08. The number was Kara's. My heart rate kicked into turbo drive. Something had happened to Zoe at dance camp.

Michael sat up and flipped on the bedside lamp. Normally, he was the one getting the calls in the dark. I hit the speakerphone.

"What happened?" I asked, not bothering to say hi.

"She's okay," Kara's voice came out in a hushed whisper. "More scared than anything."

Sitting on the edge of the bed, I rubbed sleep out of my eyes and blinked against the light.

"It's just a good thing the security guard talked to me and Jennifer first. I think we can keep this under wraps."

"Keep *what* under wraps?" Had she told me something I'd already forgotten?

Kara laughed shakily. "Sorry. I'm rattled."

"Why do you sound so strange and echoey. I can barely hear you." The hum of the AC blocked all outside noise. Yet, I had to strain to hear her.

"That's because I'm standing in the hotel stairwell. I don't want to wake anyone else. Right now, Miss Williams, Jennifer, and I are the only adults who know."

"Jennifer?"

"Jennifer Duran." The quiet Blonde.

"She and I were sitting in the coffee shop. We were scheduled to do one o'clock rounds, checking the girls' rooms, and we figured it was easier to stay up talking than go to bed beforehand. The security guard had seen us there and came to find us. He caught some of the girls sneaking out of the hotel. Seems they were heading to a bar around the corner to go dancing."

"How could they go to a bar? They're teenagers."

Kara didn't answer my stupid question. Teenage girls look a lot older when they doll up. When we were in college, Tracy and I'd loved to go out dancing before we were legally able to drink.

"He was about to wake Miss Williams, but we said we'd handle everything. I think we did. Jennifer put the fear of God into those girls. I guess she had practice with her two older boys. From what she said, they were a handful."

It was hard to imagine the unobtrusive Jennifer, who went along with everything Aimée Alterman and Kuddles Malik ever did, putting the wrath of God into anyone.

"Who was caught besides Zoe?"

She listed a half-dozen girls. All Greats. But not Jennifer's daughter, Izzy, or Emily. Relief that Kara didn't have to rescue her sweet daughter washed over me.

"They're all back in their rooms. Miss Williams is calling their parents. Zoe looked really scared. I've never seen her so upset. Too upset to talk to you tonight. Anyway, I wanted you to hear it from me and give you a heads-up before Miss Williams calls."

"Thank you." I hated to voice my next question. "Is she telling Principal Harrison?"

"We discussed that, but if she does, they could be kicked off the team."

"Maybe expelled," I said.

She fell silent a beat, then said, "They didn't actually leave the hotel, so they didn't *technically* break any rules. She's keeping it under wraps. But the girls know there won't be any second chances."

I didn't know how to thank her, not just for keeping Zoe from being expelled – it would have been one more strike against Michael's career, too – but hopefully for

scaring our daughter straight. Something had to get through
to that child.

Stumbling over thanks as best I could, I got off the
phone.

Michael looked livid.

"I'm not sure keeping this from Principal Harrison is
the right thing to do," he said the moment I'd disconnected.
"He should have the ultimate say of what goes on during
school activities."

My law and order man no matter what the cost.

I rounded on him. "Think what it would do to Zoe if
she's expelled." A horrible thought crossed my mind.
"What if the girls' scheme had worked and they'd gone to
the bar and then gotten caught? The police would be
involved!"

"Maybe if she faced some real consequences it would
wake her up to see she's messing with things that can ruin
her life." He yanked on a pair of jeans.

"You're not going to go get her, are you?" Houston
was five hours away.

His eyes snapped up to meet mine, then slid away, as
if that had been exactly what he'd been planning on. "No."
He stuffed his feet in some boots and grabbed a shirt.

"You can't be going to tell the principal."

He huffed as if I was being ridiculous. "I'm going out."

"Out where?" I called after his back as he left the

room, disappearing into the black hallway.

In the distance, a train rumbled over the crossing, its wheels screeching and whistle fading away.

He didn't come back all night.

The next morning, Michael wasn't answering my calls. I didn't hear from him until he texted me that he'd pick up Zoe when the bus arrived back at school. I'd really wanted to be there, to read her the riot act. But how could I argue with Michael in a text? Instead, I stayed at home fuming, the uncomfortable and embarrassing call with Miss Williams still echoing in my mind.

I started half a dozen chores, vacuuming, dusting, cleaning bathrooms, only to stop after a few minutes, pace to another part of the house, forgetting why I was there once I arrived. Anne hid under the bed, afraid I'd start vacuuming again. Andy followed me around for a while, thinking we were playing a game, then gave up on getting attention and went outside. Finally, late in the afternoon, I heard Michael's jeep pull into the driveway.

He dropped Zoe off but didn't come inside. She stormed past me where I stood in the kitchen chopping vegetables for a salad. I turned to say something, but she put up a hand to stop me. Her eyes were red-rimmed, her mascara smeared.

"Don't start. Daddy's already said everything that can possibly be said." She plunked something on the table and huffed from the room.

I heard her stomp up the stairs and slam her bedroom door. Christopher had already left for work. So much for family dinner. I picked up the thing she'd flung down.

It was a trophy. A golden dancer frozen on top of a faux marble column with arched back, arms up, one foot kicked over her head.

The plaque on the bottom read, "Zoe McKenzie, Outstanding Performer."

"Oh, Zoe," I said to empty air.

Chapter Thirty-One

An Altercation

Michael grounded Zoe until school started. I expected loud protests, but she never peeped. She told me the girls had talked her into going out with them to dance at a nearby club. Could I be sure they hadn't also planned to drink?

"It was stupid," she'd said. The understatement of the year.

Michael thought she'd still been trying to fit in with the older Greats.

Would she never learn? My greatest fear was she thought she'd already screwed her life up so royally that there was no reason to follow any of the rules. I'd also done some research. Substance abuse is a common reaction to sexual abuse and shame. Was she self-medicating by drinking?

Or perhaps she'd finally learned her lesson.

How was a mother to know?

We'd banned her from using computers or her phone in her room, too, so life on the surface seemed more like it used to be. We baked together, shopped for school supplies and clothes. She and I binge-watched old musicals. Christopher occasionally joined us. The two of them quit picking on each other. I wondered if Michael had filled him in on what happened at dance camp, or if her brother was just being sweet because he knew she was in trouble.

I faced up to some of my own issues, knowing I had to try and be a good role model. Kara insisted I go back to the NEST.

"You don't want to stay away forever. The enemy likes to isolate us so he can pick us off one by one. Don't fall for his tricks," she said.

She was right. Those women had prayed my family and me through a hard time already, and they were just the friends I needed to get me through what might still be coming.

Kara picked me up, so I couldn't back out. A late summer cold front had swept through the area, dropping the temperature twenty-five degrees and spattering hard drops of rain into our faces with each gust of wind. We hurried up the sidewalk.

Gabby's front door gave me flashbacks of the first

time Zoe and I'd gone back to Tracy's dance studio after the accident, and it had been Rochelle, her business partner, running things. Our grief nearly broke us. I didn't know if Zo would ever forgive me for killing her favorite person in the entire world outside of our family. Heck, Tracy *was* family. I'd felt the eyes of every parent and child in the studio watching me. Accident or not. They all blamed me. I was sure of it. I couldn't stomach the thought of what life would be like if I were indicted and then had to face the prospect of a long trial.

Now, I didn't know if I could stand an entire evening at the NEST. How could I keep from staring at where Tracy usually sat? The thought of that empty chair made me queasy. But when I walked in the door, it felt like spring had burst out in the old farm house. Every woman jumped up and hugged me as I entered. It took a few moments before I realized everything looked different, too.

Gabby saw my face and beamed.

"You did more than painting," I said gazing around.

The walls that used to be cream colored were now a soft mint shade. She'd mixed 60's-style white rattan furniture in with comfy sofas and armchairs, all in floral prints or solids in delicate peaches and greens. Compared to her home which had been a completely neutral palette before, the wash of color was fresh and bright.

"Dolores and I had a run of luck at estate sales over the

summer," Gabby said beaming. "It seemed the right time for a change."

After losing her mom, a new look probably helped even the ever-cheerful Gabby.

It would be hard to be down in such a happy setting. Besides, it looked completely different than it had a few short weeks ago when Tracy had been with us. No looking at her empty chair. Our lesson on the joy of the Lord matched the upbeat décor, and I left that evening sorry I'd waited so long to go back.

Kara chuckled when I said as much.

"Things we fear are always worse in our imaginations then when we tackle them head on."

That may be true, but there were still things looming over my life and the life of my family that I didn't want to ever face. Kara didn't know that Zoe's nude pictures might be online. Although, she was aware that at any moment I could be indicted for a felony. She tactfully never brought it up.

Once school started, we fell into our normal fall routine. As like last year, Michael and I had both the drill team and honor guard to watch during the football games. Zoe continued with her Kicker officer duties, but she didn't spend as much time at The Great's houses. Not that we would have let her after Houston, but she didn't even ask. I finally had the chance when we were alone in the car to talk to her about it.

"Aren't the girls still spending the night at The Great's?"

She shrugged and looked uncomfortable. "Yeah. They are."

"But...?" I asked, glancing her way.

"But I don't want to, so I just... just kind of let them think I'm still grounded. I hope it isn't a chicken way out, but Dad's right. I need to honor my commitment as an officer. I just don't want to be best buddies anymore." She grinned. "It helped that Madison and Layla were caught with me. They don't even question me." With a giggle, she added, "Izzy backed me up on the grounding thing, letting them think I have Draconian parents."

I laced my fingers through hers, pulled her hand up, and kissed it. Why couldn't she have told me all this weeks ago?

"Oh, Mom," she said untangling herself from my clutches.

Kara and I headed out to do some serious shopping. The local department store, Reinhardt's, which had three-story pride-of-place on the town square for 110 years was holding its fall festival, enticing people in to shop for winter clothes. Rather a laugh in north Texas where it never gets super cold.

As Dallas and Fort Worth grew, mushrooming ever closer, all the national chains marched up the highway towards us. Graitney's center of stately old buildings and homes was surrounded now by carbon copy strip malls and identical subdivisions. Family businesses struggled to compete even before the behemoth Amazon became part of the mix. However, the folks of Graitney believed in supporting their local businesses.

We finished at Reinhardt's, each carrying an armload of bags full of bargains we couldn't resist. We were debating where to eat lunch when my phone rang. I tapped it on without noticing the number.

"Mrs. McKenzie," a male voice I didn't recognize said. "This is Principal Harrison. Could you come to the school as quickly as possible?"

An ominous feeling instantly clouded the sunny fall day. We were only a few weeks into the school year. What had Zoe done now?

"Your son, Christopher, has been in an altercation."

I heard nothing else he said. It made no sense. Other than the rare times he and his sister picked on one another, Christopher had never been in a fight. His size intimidated most of the other kids, but more than that, my son was too easy-going. Nothing rattled him. Nothing made him mad.

Ever.

What in the world could have happened?

Throwing my bags into the car, I told Kara there was an emergency at school and tore off, breaking every speed limit between downtown and the campus on the edge of town. Thank goodness none of Michael's patrol cars spotted me. He had enough going on.

Had the school called him, too?

As I pulled into visitor parking, I got my answer. His Jeep sat parked in the emergency lane, portable flashers rotating on the roof. Groaning, I jumped out of the car and raced up the broad stairs leading to the front doors. Before I hit the buzzer on the video monitor to be let inside, Mrs. Garcia, the school secretary with whom I'd worked many times at various school functions, opened the door for me.

"Oh, Sheena. This is all your poor family needs right now," she said.

"Do you know what happened?"

She shook her head and led the way down the hall and into the front office. "No idea. I just heard a fight broke out in the cafeteria. I'd never in a million years believe your boy was involved. He's got the nicest manners of any child at school."

Mrs. Garcia led me through the outer area and stopped outside the principal's office, the solid wood door closed. An excited voice came from inside, answered by the deep, steady tone of my husband. Just hearing his familiar rumble dropped my heartrate from overdrive to first gear.

I knocked, then pushed on the door when someone said to come in.

The good-sized space felt crowded with all the people gathered there. Light streaming through widows that opened onto the school's courtyard highlighted anxious faces. Everyone looked nervous except Michael. What I assumed to be the family of the other kid squashed together on a tweed sofa along one side of the room. A mom, her face a slightly green shade; a dad, looking murderous; and a muscular boy with a bloody washrag pressed to his nose, all looked up when I entered.

Christopher jumped up and gestured for me to sit in his chair. He lifted an ice pack back to his eye, which was swollen shut and turning a bruised looking reddish-purple color. Michael glanced at me, his cop face on. I couldn't read any expression.

When I sat down, Mr. Harrison said, "To catch you up Mrs. McKenzie, your son and his classmate, Marcus Simpson, were in a physical altercation during their lunch period."

"I can see that."

A thin man, with only a fringe of fine brown hair stood behind the principal's chair wringing his hands. "I'm Curtis Clayton, Vice-principal and lunch monitor. I witnessed the entire figh…altercation. As the children were eating their lunches, Marcus approached Christopher."

On the sofa, the boy's dad bowed up, and the small teacher instinctively shrunk back. He took a steadying breath and forged ahead, "I surmise, he made some nasty personal accusations. Christopher started to stand, but Marcus took a swing before your son had gotten to his feet."

The Vice-principal flicked a glance toward Michael. "Caught him a good one across his eye."

"Is there any doubt that Marcus threw the first punch?" I asked.

Both the teacher and the principal shook their heads.

The small teacher shot a nervous glance at the family on the sofa. "There is an entire roomful of eyewitnesses," he answered

"Wait one minute," Mr. Simpson, a barrel-chested man, who looked like he'd once played football but let the muscle go to fat, lumbered to his feet and pointed at Michael.

"My son says your boy provoked him." He glared down at my husband with a mulish expression, as if daring him to stand up and fight.

Michael remained seated, looking back steadily. "From the witnesses' accounts I've already collected," he tapped the small notebook on his lap, "and what the surveillance recording will undoubtedly show, Marcus should be arrested for committing assault causing bodily injury."

"What about zero tolerance?" Mr. Simpson growled. "Doesn't that make both boys at fault?"

"In this school district, zero tolerance does not apply in clear cases of self-defense," Principal Harrison explained.

Michael continued as if he hadn't been interrupted. "Marcus is looking at a Class A misdemeanor. He's eighteen and an adult, so this could result in him spending one year in county jail and charged a $4,000 fine."

Mrs. Simpson made a horrified squawk, and Mr. Simpson slid down onto the couch again.

"However," Michael paused, using a practiced ploy to let the reality of what he said sink in, "after Christopher is examined by a physician, and the extent of his injuries determined—"

"He broke my son's nose," Mr. Simpson shouted, sitting upright.

"Self-defense." Christopher muttered.

I'd never heard my son be so short with an adult. I chanced a glance his way. He backed against the wall and let out a breath, his shoulders dropping, forcing himself to relax. If the young Simpson was anything like the senior, I didn't blame Christopher for being angry.

"As I was saying," Michael went on, titanium strength evident beneath the velvet voice, "we will readdress the issue once the full extent of Marcus's culpability and the damages are determined. Principal Harrison and I will decide, partially depending on Marcus's school record, whether this matter can be left to school disciplinary measures or if it has crossed the line into a police matter."

He stood and it was the Simpson family who shrank back, trying to melt into the couch cushions.

Michael nodded toward the principal who sat upright behind the broad expanse of his desk, clasping hands which shook slightly. "Mr. Harrison, I'll be in touch."

Christopher and I followed Michael from the room. Mrs. Garcia flickered a sad smile as we passed. We didn't speak as we walked out of the school. On the front steps, Michael told our son to go get in my car.

Then he turned to me, "Let me know what the emergency clinic says. I'm worried he might have a fractured cheek or eye socket. He'll need an MRI. Be sure to monitor him for concussion." Michael strode down the steps, yanked open his car door, grabbed the flasher off the roof, slammed the door, and peeled away.

No kiss. No good-bye or see-you-later. Not the slightest hint of my husband under the cop facade. I could have been any old citizen at any old crime scene. Certainly not his wife.

"All right, buster." I slammed my own door after skootching into the driver's seat. "Fess up. I don't think I've ever seen your dad so mad."

"I know. Even Old Homer Simpson was quaking in his size fourteens."

I nearly grinned, but Christopher wasn't getting off that easily. "Seriously, I want the whole story." Putting the car in gear, I looked over my shoulder and pulled out. "What did that jerk say about Zoe?"

"Huh? Who said something about Zoe?"

Glancing over, I saw he wasn't trying to be cute. Christopher had no idea what I was talking about.

"I thought the fight was about Marcus saying something mean."

He squirmed and tried to slink lower in the seat, but at six foot, four inches, that didn't really work. "Yeah...he did."

Nothing else. Was I going to have to pull every word out of him? It felt like the time he fell into a cactus while playing outside at my grandparents' house when he was three. Papa had been so patient pulling every slender, silver thorn out of Christopher's delicate flesh, the poor boy cringing but bravely not crying as each barb slid out.

"Tell me. What did he say that made you so mad?"

Christopher's hazel eyes looked as sad as our old lab's used to when he got in trouble for chewing socks.

"You might as well tell me. Your dad will when he gets home." I swung the car into the parking lot of the emergency clinic.

Graitney's only hospital was antiquated, the reason serious cases like mine went to large hospitals in Dallas or Fort Worth. For minor injuries, the gleaming-brick and shiny-windowed twenty-four-hour emergency clinic had been a godsend.

I turned off the car but didn't get out, just looked at Christopher.

His eyes darted to me and then out the window. "Marcus said you were a drunk who killed everybody's favorite dance teacher. That all the kids hate you."

The ringing in my ears was the oxygen being sucked from the car.

I struggled to breath. Could barely speak. "What...what did you say?"

Staring out the windshield, Christopher said, "I called him a liar, of course." His gaze fell to his fists clenched in his lap, icepack forgotten. "I tried to stand up, but he decked me before I could get to my feet."

My sweet, good-natured boy, whom everyone got along with and loved, finally looked at me and smiled. "Then I broke his nose."

Chapter Thirty-Two

New Mission, Old Friend

Thankfully, Christopher sustained no injuries other than a nasty black eye. The school suspended the Simpson kid, but the police took no action. The dust-up seemed to stop other kids from saying things to Christopher about me.

At least as far as I knew.

Michael regained his normal calm by that evening, although he and Christopher spent forty-five minutes together in the study having a serious discussion. Neither one told me what they talked about, but I just happened to be passing by a couple of times and heard Michael say something about the importance of keeping your temper and never throwing the first punch.

With soccer and Kicker practice, dance classes, and Honor guard, not to mention studying, the kids were busy.

Michael was too as he put in extra hours trying to figure out who was doing the sextortion. Even with her crazy schedule, and over my objections, Zoe started helping him.

I hated what they were doing together, but I also knew it was vital. Vital to Michael and the FBI's investigation, at least. At what cost to Zoe? In the evenings, she and her dad poured through the garbage on the predator's computer to see if Zoe could find any connection to herself. It might be the key to discovering the sicko's identity. Even though all they could see were the poor kids' faces, the essential spark and energy that had always been part of my daughter faded more each day. Would there be any light left in her by the time they finished?

Other than scratches, scrapes, bruises, and the occasional broken bone, raising Christopher had been so easy. The fight at school had literally been the only time he'd ever been in trouble. And I could hardly blame *him* for that one. I loved Zoe dearly, but it seemed I spent all my time worrying about her.

Hearing Michael's footsteps on the kitchen tiles, I pulled my mind from the rolling hills of south Texas and historical reenactors. A world scrumptiously recreated by my favorite author, Kit Hawthorne. Her hill country romances had become my means of escape. Anne, curled up in my lap, and I both lifted our heads. Zoe looking haggard trailed into the house behind Michael.

"How did it go?" I asked. As if they'd tell me anything.

"About the same," Michael grunted, as he rooted around in the fridge.

Zoe shuffled across the living room and collapsed into an armchair. She shivered and unconsciously gave her hands a quick shake, as if trying to shake off what she'd seen. Even though they viewed only faces, it would be hard not to think of the filth the victims were subject to.

Flopping her head back against the cushion, Zoe closed her eyes. "Some of those poor kids are so young. I can't get their huge eyes out of my head." She sighed. "Maybe I never will."

Michael stood in the doorway, Dr. Pepper in hand. I shot him an angry look.

We'd had quite the knock-down drag-out about him letting her do this. I was dead-set against it.

"Hasn't she been through enough already!" I railed at him.

"Zoe wants to help," he insisted. "Maybe it will bring closure."

"Or years of PTSD," I'd muttered wanting to get in the final word.

Sometimes being right stinks.

"Oh, sweetie. You know you don't have to do this."

She shook her head, not opening her eyes. "Yes, I do. It's the only way he doesn't win. We've got to stop him."

"Maybe you should let the trained people handl—"

"Mom!" Zoe snapped upright like a Jack-in-the-box. "We've been through this. I'm not a little kid."

I swallowed.

"Not anymore. He took that. And I'll *never* let him take innocence from another child." She bolted from the room.

Michael looked over at me, but before he could say a word, I buried my head back in the book. We'd gotten good at ignoring one another.

Just as I really began to despair for my daughter who seemed so unhappy, she surprised me yet again. Zoe climbed into the car following an extra Kicker practice on Friday afternoon about a month after school had started. She looked hot. Dark curls pulled loose from her ponytail curled around her flushed face.

"How did it go?"

"Um…okay."

She pitched her dance bag in the back seat and fastened her seatbelt. "Can we go get a hot fudge sundae at Polly Sue's?"

"It's pretty close to dinnertime."

"Please, Mom."

Something in her tone made me hesitate. Besides, between school, dance, Kicker practices, homework, and the help she'd been giving her dad it had been awhile since we'd had any alone time.

"Sure. Why not?" I put the car in gear.

Football games varied between Thursday and Friday nights until the playoffs. If the team got that far, there were Saturday games thrown into the mix. The playoffs seemed like they might be a possibility this year. The Graitney Giants had a strong team. During the game the night before, they had romped the opposing team. The football playoffs ran into December, and so far, the Giants looked on track to go to the state championships for 4A schools. The extra Kicker practices were to work on holiday routines just in case.

"The girls are going to spend the night at the Alterman's tonight," she said in a flat voice.

My stomach clenched.

Was she going to ask to join them? Had she changed her mind about staying close friends? Maybe she felt pressured...or left out again.

As an officer, Zoe needed to get along with the other girls. Still, Michael and I really didn't want her going. She wasn't grounded anymore, and I liked to think there was adult supervision at those houses so that what happened at camp wouldn't happen here in town.

I mulled over what to say as I drove, and she fiddled with the radio finding a station she liked better than the classical music already playing.

We parked in the lot of the old-fashioned ice cream shop and stepped out into air so thick with humidity that it wrapped around us and clung like a wet blanket. We scurried to the shade of the awning over the front. When we pushed open the shop door, it felt as if we stepped into a freezer. We Texans love our AC.

The cloying smells of vanilla and sugar washed over us, along with a rush of memories. We'd spent a lot of time there throughout the kids' childhoods. Polly Sue's had always been their favorite reward for a completing the chore chart, scooping the poop in the backyard, and not killing one another on cross-country family vacations.

An antique soda fountain ran down one wall behind which three workers dropped enormous balls of frozen goodness into homemade waffle cones. Sweetheart-style parlor chairs surrounded tiny tables on the black and white checkerboard floor. We studied the large blackboard which listed over fifty flavors – a silly ritual because we always got the same thing. I ordered a waffle cone with one scoop of After Dinner Mint Chocolate Chip, and Zoe got a hot fudge sundae.

She took a seat at a table with a view of the entrance. I noticed her darting anxious glances that way every time the door opened and wondered who she was waiting for. Zoe sat stiffly, obviously tense. It made me nervous and I didn't have a clue why.

"Tell me what routines you girls are working on?" I asked, hoping to distract her.

She swung her attention to me, eager as always to talk about dance.

"We've got the coolest number for October set to Michael Jackson's 'Thriller.' It will be so awesome. Today we started work on a holiday medley with songs like 'I Saw Mommy Kissing Santa Claus.' We're going to wear Santa hats and cute red dresses with white fur collars and cuffs. If there's a solo, I'm going to tryout."

I loved that she had normal things planned for the future.

"So far, my squad is doing great. Some of the other squads are struggling getting the routines down."

Zoe filled me in on all the details, but she ate slowly and kept darting looks at the door. I tried to savor my own ice cream as I wondered who she expected. A boy? One of The Greats? Some kid I didn't know who might bring on a whole new set of problems? I was being ridiculous and paranoid.

Suddenly, her eyes lit up. She quit talking, her expression tentative. I didn't want to be obvious, so I turned just a little and glanced out of the corner of my eye.

Kara and Emily strolled through the door.

My insides churned like an old-fashioned ice cream maker. I desperately wanted the girls to make up. Since Zoe had finagled us being here, I hoped that she wanted it too, but would Emily?

I gave Kara a jaunty wave. She changed course, scooted around the packed tables, and made her way towards us. Emily followed. Reluctantly? I tried to read her body language.

"Why don't you join us?" I asked.

Zoe seemed to be holding her breath. Neither girl looked at the other.

"Sure," Kara said too brightly. She wanted things back to normal as much as I did. We talked about it every time we were together. "That would be great. Why don't you sit down, Em. I'll go get you a sundae. Extra nuts, right?"

Before her daughter could decline, Kara hurried away. Emily sat down and sent me a shy smile. I noticed she wore the translucent pendant and earrings I'd made for her last birthday. They changed color depending on the light. My heart filled with warmth. I'd never dream of making The Greats special jewelry. I didn't think they'd appreciate a gift that came wrapped in love not a Tiffany's box.

An awkward silent beat passed. Both girls avoided looking at each other. Emily fussed with hanging her purse on the back of the chair, then couldn't find a place to put her arms. The wiry arms of the chair seemed uncomfortable, so she crossed her arms, seemed to think better of that, and rested them awkwardly on her legs. Zoe let her ice cream melt while she nonchalantly watched Kara place the ice cream order.

"Zoe was just telling me about the new routines," I said to Emily, trying to break the ice. "They sound great. She said you have a solo during 'Thriller.' Congratulations. That's super impressive."

Zoe flicked a grateful look my way.

In no time, Kara was back and the girls were eating and talking about dance as if they'd never had a fight. The tension melted away like a dropped fudgesicle. Kara grinned between every bite. When we finished, she glanced at her watch and laughed.

"I keep thinking I need to get home, but Eric is out of town at the National Newspaper Association annual convention."

"Why don't you and Emily come over to eat?" I asked impulsively. "Michael is working late. Christopher is gone, too. We could make it a girls' night. Order pizza and watch a movie. We've been saving *Funny Face* for a night when the guys are gone."

"That would be awesome," Emily said.

The movie was one of the girls' favorites.

"Could Emily spend the night?" Zoe asked.

"Sure." I noticed Zoe already had her phone out.

"I'll text Madison and tell her something's come up and I can't come over."

Young friendship is amazing. It was as if Emily and Zoe had never had a disagreement. They were back to spending every waking moment together, this time joined by Isabella Duran – Izzy. Out of The Greats, I'd always liked Izzy best. Perhaps my judgement was biased because I'd often felt for her quiet mother, Jennifer, who never seemed to quite fit in with The Blondes. Izzy was also quiet. She had polite manners like the other Greats, but unlike them, she would hang out and talk to me, which went a long way in winning me over. Besides, she complimented my jewelry and asked to see my studio. I studied her creamy complexion thinking how pretty something in shades of amber and gold would look with her brunette hair and coffee-colored eyes.

Being around the three of them, it was clear the quiet Great fit in a lot better with my girls than she had with her more flamboyant former besties. It turned out her family were devoted Catholics, and faith was an essential part of their home life. I liked that. It made me happy to have the house filled with the shrieks and giggles of teenaged girls again, and I realized how empty it had seemed when Zoe spent so much time at other people's homes over the summer.

"Paige has sort of taken her place in The Great hierarchy," Zoe explained to me on the way to dance a couple of weeks later when I asked about it. "Izzy's cool. She doesn't feel like she has to change who she is just to fit in."

I waited a beat to see where Zoe was going with that thought.

"She's like Emily that way…and me, now. I hope. I did some super dumb things trying to be liked by the wrong people."

I prayed she really understood that and had changed.

Even with my legal troubles and concern over Zoe's pictures still looming over our family, things felt brighter. My daughter seemed to be finding her way again.

The next Saturday night, the three girls had gone out for burgers and then to the latest super hero movie. I was to pick them up at 11:15. Em and Izzy were spending the night with Zoe afterward. Michael and I spent a rare evening at home. He grilled steaks and veggies. While not yet cool, the late summer heat had broken, and we ate on the patio by the pool. We'd both been under so much stress we desperately needed to reconnect.

Michael must have felt the same way because without

discussing it, we kept our conversation to things going on around town not within our family. The fall roses' heavy perfume struck just the right note against the moldy damp smell of wet earth and succulent grilled meat. The insect chorus grew louder as the sun set. We were in a glorious glass bubble, perfect and precious. I wished we never had to leave.

For the first time in weeks, I felt close to my husband. Michael put a warm hand on the back of my neck, his big fingers massaging deeply, and I sighed back into the pressure. Massages were one of the many things he did well.

"If we move upstairs," he said, his voice a low rumble, "we have time for some *dessert* before we have to pick up the girls."

I put a hand over his. "I like your thinking."

We stood up and gathered the dishes. Just as we reached the patio door, his phone started playing the Hawaii 5-0 theme song, his work ring. It always made people smile, but I wanted to snatch the thing from his hand and pitch it into the pool.

"Chief McKenzie," he said, answering.

Laying down what I carried, I took the platter and tongs from his hand, straining to hear the other side of the conversation. All Michael did was grunt and "uh-huh."

"Okay. I'm on my way," he said and clicked off. He

looked as disappointed as I felt. "Sorry, She-Girl. I've got to go."

"Why? What's happened?"

Michael hesitated, then shrugged. "You'll hear about it anyway. Patrol rounded up a group of Kickers and football players. Probably a DWI and some consumption of alcohol by minors. I'd better be at the station when their parents start arriving."

My hand flew to my throat. "Is Zoe…is she one of…"

"Not that I know. Although given what happened at camp…," he stopped and shook his head. "Let's give her the benefit of the doubt until we hear something else, okay?"

Chapter Thirty-Three

How The Mighty Have Fallen

Michael gave me a quick kiss before heading off to grab his stuff. He turned at the foot of the stairs. "Raincheck?"

I tried to nod and smile, not sure I pulled it off.

For the next few hours, I kept glancing at my phone, but no calls came in from Zoe or Michael, leading me to assume she was safely at the movies. Even so, my heart beat hard as I waited outside the theater to pick up the girls. A wave of relief washed over me when I saw Zoe's glossy-black, Emily's rose-gold, and Izzy's deep-brown heads bent together talking as they exited the theater. They all stared down at one of their phones.

"How was the show?" I asked as they climbed into the car.

"Good."

"Fine."

"Great, Mrs. M."

"Did you hear what happened tonight, Mom?" Zoe rode shotgun, and I gave her a quick peek before pulling out of the parking space.

"The Kickers and football players being stopped for DWI and underage drinking?" I asked.

She nodded. "I figured Dad told you."

"How do you girls know, already?"

All three gave uncomfortable chuckles.

"Our phones blew up during the entire movie," Emily said.

Zoe added, "We did more texting than watching the show."

I could imagine.

"What did you learn?" I asked, as anxious to know what had been happening as they were.

"Three senior Kickers and their boyfriends were caught doing ninety on the highway. The patrolman who pulled them over smelled alcohol," Zoe said. "The driver failed the field sobriety tests. Totally wasted."

Emily took up the story, "Stupid kids had an open tequila bottle in the car, too. They all got taken to the station."

"They weren't in an accident?" I asked. The

nightmares about my accident flashed in my mind's eye. "No one was hurt?"

"No, Mrs. M," Emily said. "They are all okay. Just in a lot of trouble."

"Who are they?"

They rattled off the names. The boys I knew only from the football roster. I'd never met them. I knew the girl, Hailey Cuthbertson, a curvy senior Kicker, only from years of watching dance shows. Zoe had never been close friends with her.

However, Layla Malek and Madison Alterman were another matter altogether. As the Kicker's team captain and one of the senior lieutenants, they were supposed to set an example for the entire team. As their moms were fond of reminding the rest of us.

Some example...not that our family could throw stones.

"Hope Layla and Maddy aren't mad at you, Zo," Izzy said.

"Why?" Zoe asked before I could ask the same question.

What did my daughter have to do with them breaking the law? She wasn't even with them this time.

"They think having you around is like a good luck charm," Izzy explained. "That if they do something wrong, they won't get busted."

Zoe whipped around so fast the end of her hair slapped me across the face. "What?"

"That's not the only reason they like you," Izzy added quickly, a note of apology in her voice. "It's just an extra benefit of having you for a friend."

"They think they won't get in trouble because of my dad?" Zoe snorted. "They sure don't know him." She turned back around, crossing her arms. "Some friends they are."

The rest of the drive, the girls talked about the changes that would happen to the football and dance teams. Arrest for drinking was a clear violation of school rules. Only one of the boys was in a critical football position as a tight end, but the girls thought a certain junior would be able to step up. As for the Kickers, Madison and Layla would be kicked off the team for sure.

I wondered if Zoe realized how close she'd come to the same fate with her exploits at dance camp over the summer. Perhaps covering that up had emboldened the other girls. Layla and Madison had been part of the group caught sneaking out of the hotel.

Maybe they thought Zoe's dad had pulled strings then.

They discussed if Miss Williams would choose new officers or if the current ones would simply move up in rank. That would make Izzy team captain.

At least Zoe hadn't been foolish enough to drink and

drive. I shuddered. Thank goodness, her nut hadn't fallen that close to my twisted tree.

Michael arrived home shortly after we did. The girls set up air mattresses on the family room floor and snuggled into sleeping bags in front of the television. The scent of popcorn and the sound of urgent whispers and a laugh track followed us upstairs. I carried two mugs of hot chocolate from the crockpot full I'd made for the girls.

He kicked off his boots, emptied his pockets, and joined me in the sitting area of our bedroom. I handed him the marshmallow and chocolate scented brew. "How did it turn out?"

"The driver is charged with DWI, the other five with consumption of alcohol by a minor." Michael sighed and sipped the cocoa before setting it down. He looked exhausted.

"Rough night."

He rubbed the back of his hand over his jaw. "You could say that. Six sets of irate parents threatening to sue, to take the poor patrolman's badge, and run me out of town on a rail." He shook his head. "That lady with the silly name…"

"Kuddles Malik?"

"Yeah, her. If ever a nickname didn't fit a person."

I sniffed. "We've always assumed it's to be taken as irony."

"Well, she's a piece of work."

"She's bad enough with petty school issues. I can't imagine how she'd act when something serious has happened to her child." I sipped my chocolate.

"I can tell you." Michael stretched out his long legs. "She yelled at everyone within sight, but it's her husband I'm more worried about."

I arched an eyebrow at him over the mug.

"He's a hotshot Dallas lawyer. When those kids got busted last year, he and his cohorts managed to get them off with a slap on the wrist. He's determined to do it again. But tonight's incident is a lot more serious, and these kids need to realize it. The driver blew a point one six."

"Isn't that twice the legal limit?"

You'd think with all that I'd been going through I'd know all this, but I'd been pretty out of it when the lawyer explained it to me at the hospital, and since then, I'd tried my best to not think about it.

"Right. The legal limit for a BAC, blood alcohol concentration, is point oh eight, a Class B Misdemeanor. For an adult, point one five is a Class A. In Texas, however, if a minor tests positive for *any* blood-alcohol at all they're charged with a DUI, a Class C, which can be bumped up to a DWI depending on their BAC."

I nodded as he reeled all this off.

"So, the driver got a DWI and an open container

violation. The passengers get consumption of alcohol by a minor. Easy to prove as they were drinking and are under twenty-one."

"So how did those kids get off last year?" I asked.

"Good lawyers, one of which was Layla's dad." Michael's lips parted in a smile with no warmth. "But they are two very different cases. The kids last year were busted at a party, not driving. They got off with a fine and community service. Drunk driving is a much more serious offense."

He said all this clinically, as if explaining it to a class of rookie police cadets, but memories of what happened to Tracy crashed down on me.

I slumped back in the chair. "I know."

The relief I'd felt at learning Zoe wasn't in trouble again disappeared under the weight of my own issues. I didn't need any reminder that I could be facing jail time myself soon.

It's the oddest sensation. Even though one's life may be crumbling around them like a sand castle in a tsunami, life goes on. Night follows day. Seasons change. Other people go about their jobs, school, sports. Whenever I'd let myself obsess over what might happen to me or Zoe, or worry about Michael's job, I'd look around amazed that the rest of the world could be acting so normally.

One of those times happened the next week while I stood talking to Tracy's business partner. Though Rochelle must have been broken-hearted at losing her friend, she had done an excellent job of running the *Heart For Dance* studio since Tracy's death. Life goes on. I didn't know a lot about Rochelle other than she was a cousin of the high school dance team teacher Miss Williams, who'd first introduced her to Tracy.

Outwardly, she and my friend could not have been more different. Tracy dressed flamboyantly. Rochelle traditionally. Tracy had pale skin and straight blonde hair, tipped fuchsia. Caramel-toned Rochelle wore her hair in short chocolate twists. Tracy loud. Rochelle soft-spoken. Tracy straw-thin. Rochelle curvaceous.

Inwardly, they could be the same person. They believed dance made the world a better place, and they loved their dancers fiercely.

She'd been nothing but kind to me after the accident. I worried about her reaction almost more than anyone else's when the truth came out about what had happened that night. Because she'd been so dear to Tracy, I couldn't stand the thought of seeing condemnation in her eyes.

I pushed the thoughts aside and thanked her again for fitting Zoe in for extra rehearsal time. The Kickers were auditioning for a solo during the playoff game in AT&T Stadium where the Dallas Cowboys play, if the Giants made it that far.

Zoe wanted the part desperately.

"It's no problem, Mrs. McKenzie. Zoe's a talented dancer. Tracy was so proud of her."

I swallowed hard.

"I'm just happy she didn't let that Layla and Madison rub off on her," Rochelle continued. "Imagine them being arrested for underage drinking. And their being Kicker officers, too! Thank goodness, the school took those positions away and gave them to the good girls – Isabella, your Zoe, and Emily. They'll do the Kickers proud."

I hoped the fixed smile on my face didn't give me away. What I'd done to this kind woman was horrible enough. I prayed she'd never learn about my daughter's dirty secrets. Her good opinion was too important.

She didn't seem to notice anything wrong, just kept talking, "That dance team needs officers they can look up to. I've never heard so much bad talk going on with all the girls. Even the little bitty ones here at the studio know Layla and Madison did something wrong. At least, we don't have to deal with them here any longer. Their folks pulled them out of the studio. Heard they're taking classes in another town. Wouldn't surprise me if next year they change schools, too. It's a shame the school didn't expel them, but they weren't arrested on campus or at a school function. So, I guess they couldn't be."

Everyone in town had become knowledgeable about school rules since Madison, Layla, Hailey, and the three football players' spectacular fall from grace. As usual, Michael had been right; Mr. Malik and his cohorts had not been able to make these charges go away. Not that he wasn't still trying.

A part of me hurt for the kids' parents, even though some of the moms weren't very pleasant. We all wanted the best for our kids.

Zoe came out of the restroom after changing clothes and skipped up to us.

"Thanks for helping me, Miss Rochelle. I feel a lot more comfortable with that combination now," she said.

"You'll do great, hon. I've got every confidence in you."

I could have kissed Rochelle for stepping into Tracy's dance shoes. She had no idea how much my daughter needed someone to believe in her right now.

Zoe beamed.

Chapter Thirty-Four

On The Rocks

Zoe *did* seem to be doing well now that she and Emily had made up, and I was grateful. I wished the same held true for my marriage.

Married nearly twenty years, we'd never felt further apart. With everything that had happened during our life together – and with Michael's job in law enforcement, there had been some heartbreaking times – we'd pulled together and found strength from our faith and one another. Now that we were dealing with so many issues, it was all we could do to keep the plates spinning in the air, especially Michael.

Things had seemed better, but it had only been a temporary reprieve. I knew it wasn't true, but it felt like not only had God turned his back on me but so had my husband. Day by day, we grew further apart. Each one of us dealing with everything as best we could but sadly not as a team.

As we entered October, our lawyer said we might be getting the lab results back soon, if he could expedite things. Texas forensics labs had long backlogs. Suddenly, the giant clock counting down in my mind sped up. The FBI and Michael hadn't made any progress in identifying the sextortionist. The burden of that responsibility, along with everything else, seemed to weigh down my husband. I had a nagging feeling something else was going on, too. I just couldn't put my finger on it.

Gone were the days of gruff, warm humor.

No one from the outside would have seen anything amiss. In fact, we were probably politer to one another than we'd ever been. But it was an icy layer carefully laid over daily life. Frost on the edge of a pond so brittle I worried the smallest, chance-thrown pebble might shatter it.

"Would you like some more toast?" I asked Michael at breakfast, my hand hovering over the dish, impatient for him to finish and get out of the house so I could attend my daily pity party. A bad habit that I had neither an idea how nor the will power to break.

He'd been staring at his phone since he sat down and only grunted noncommittally to my feeble attempts at conversation. He didn't answer or seem to be aware I loomed beside him. I tried to see what was so fascinating on the screen but could only surmise it was a text from work. Probably not good news.

"Toast?" I raised my voice this time and he jumped, startled.

"Huh?"

"Toast? Would you like more toast?"

Michael's gaze swept up over me, down to his plate, and then back to me. "No, thanks." He shoved back his chair, thumbing off the phone. "I'm fine. Thank you."

Four long strides took him to the counter where he swept up his keys.

Half way out the door, he turned as if remembering something. "Ah...Thank you for breakfast."

His frowning gaze and entire focus were somewhere other than our kitchen where the morning light made the walls glow daffodil-yellow.

"I don't know when I'll be home."

The door swished shut behind him before I could answer. As if he wanted an answer. No kiss. No see-you-later, or I'll-call-you-later. No breakfast really either. I picked up his untouched plate of cold eggs and tipped it into the trash. As hard as it was to believe, something else must have happened. I leaned back against the counter.

Please, God, we can't take anything else.

Kara's ringtone, Here Comes the Sun, played on my

phone, and I pulled it out of my pants pocket.

I didn't even manage to say hi before she started talking, "Oh, Sheena, I'm so sorry. I can't believe it! Your poor family. Will the bad news ever stop? How is Michael handling it?"

My back scrapped along the edge of the counter as I sank to the floor.

"Sheena? Honey? Are you still there?"

What? What's happened now? My mind screamed but I couldn't form words. My brain, still fragile, recoiled. My vision telescoped down to a tiny grey pinpoint. Kara must have heard me hyperventilating. My phone cracked hard against tile floor as it fell.

"Hold on, Honey," her voice sounded tiny and far away. "Don't move. I'll be there in a minute."

A minute? Twenty? Ten? Time did its strange stretchy thing again like it had after the accident.

The door to the backyard patio slid open and Kara called out, "The side gate was unlocked. I came in that way. Are you oka…?"

Her words cut off abruptly, and she hurried over to me. My vision washed back into wavering focus. Her bright hair spilled from a messy ponytail on top of her head. The sun streaming through the large window highlighted the loose curly strands like a shining golden halo.

"My guardian angel," I said without humor.

She reached down and pulled me to my feet. A guardian angel who looked horrified. Kara gripped my arm and shoved me towards the breakfast table, helping me get seated. She looked halfway dressed: make up, jewelry, and a sleeveless shirt on but still wearing the flannel pants she slept in.

"Can I get you something to drink? Water? Coffee? Tea?" She giggled a little hysterically. "I sound like a flight attendant. A doctor? Do you need to go to the doctor? Did you pass out? Did you have a relapse?"

She looked so frightened I finally found my voice. "No. I didn't pass out. I don't need a doctor. I need you to sit down." I shoved dirty dishes out of the way. "Sit down and tell me what you were talking about on the phone. What's happened now?"

Kara slid into a chair, her face so pale only the sunburned tip of her nose glowed making me think of Rudolph. I must be losing it.

I clamped a hand on her arm. "Something was wrong with Michael this morning, but he didn't tell me what. It's him, isn't it?"

"Oh, Sheena. He should be the one to tell you, not me...." She ran her free hand through her hair making the halo fluffier. "But since I've already put my foot in my mouth, I guess I have to tell you."

She took a steadying breath and said, "The mayor is

set to announce that he's looking for someone to replace
Michael as chief of police."

Chapter Thirty-Five

Sage Advice

Kara filled me in on everything she'd learned from Eric, who had sources in the mayor's office. Michael served "at the mayor's pleasure" and theoretically, he could be removed from office at any time.

"But Michael and Mayor Waverly have always had a good relationship," I said, mostly to reassure myself.

"True." Her hand clasped a long, teardrop-shaped pendant I'd made for her birthday. The iridescent, peach-colored glass looked gorgeous with her hair. She held it tightly, zipping it back and forth on its chain. "But the mayor's a politician through and through. He must have been hearing things from his constituents."

Immediately, my mind ran through likely people. We'd lived in Graitney for eighteen years and prided ourselves on being on good terms with most everyone. Who could do such a thing? Michael was a great at his job. Who would want him out?

Get real.

After what I'd done, who wouldn't? Who thinks it's not a problem if the chief of police's wife is arrested for drunk driving and felony manslaughter? Then if news about Zoe's photos leaked out, add to that Christopher breaking a student's nose, we might as well pack up and move.

Kara stared at me with a worried frown. *Zip. Zip.* "What are you thinking? I don't like that dark look in your eyes." More zipping.

"I'm thinking I need to move. Far away. Michael does a wonderful job as chief. It's not his fault I messed everything up."

Her shoulders drooped. "Oh, honey. What do you mean? You were in an accident plain and simple. Your arrest was only law enforcement following protocol. That's all. At least until you know something different." *Zip. Zip.* "Leave Michael? You'd never leave him, Sheena. And what about the kids? Would they stay or would you take them? Where would you go?"

I flashed her a defeated look.

Kara pushed the pendant against her lips, as if trying to keep herself from saying something she'd regret.

More guilt flooded me, she only meant to help.

Noticing what she was doing, Kara lifted the necklace and looked at it. "What would you do, Sheena? Can you support yourself making jewelry?"

"Ha. Not hardly. It's a nice side business, but it would never support me and the kids."

Even thinking of such a thing overwhelmed me. Tears pricked my eyes and I cleared my throat. "Really, Kara. What *am* I going to do?"

She let the necklace go and sat up straight, grasping my hand. "You are going to talk to your husband and quit thinking these silly thoughts. You're my best friend, and I hate to say it," she sighed, "but you need to quit wallowing in self-pity."

"I'm no—" I began.

She snorted and hit me with a steely glare.

I slumped back in the chair, our hands released. "Okay, I am, but it's not like I don't have good reason."

"Of course, you've got good reason, but that's not a good excuse. You're an adult and a mom and a *wife!* What happened to putting others first?"

She had me there. My own problems consumed my thoughts.

"Maybe my leaving would be putting them first." I knew it was a lie even as I said it. Zoe needed me more than ever before in her life. Kara didn't even know that sordid storyline, although she and Eric knew we were waiting to hear about the felony indictment. And obviously, the mayor knows about it, too.

"Michael might be glad to see me go." I crossed my arms. "It would certainly make his life easier."

"Sheena, you don't really believe that, do you? Where's the 'for better or worse?'"

"We could do with a little better," I mumbled toward the table top.

Kara scowled. "Jeesh!"

Her normally buoyant face crumpled, looking disappointed. I'd made a mess of everything in my life. I didn't want to damage our friendship, too.

"What would you do if you were me?" I asked, begging.

"Talk to my husband." Her tone brooked no argument. "Support him."

I couldn't bring myself to tell her Michael and I weren't exactly baring our souls to one another right now. I felt more like an isolated ice-maiden than a helpmeet.

"He's certainly been supportive of you. I've never seen a man more stricken with concern for his wife than Michael was for you after the accident. He barely left your side. I don't think he slept until you were out of the hospital. He really hasn't been himself since."

Her words were whips lashing my conscience,

highlighted by the sound of the pendant zipping back and forth on the chain again. And she only knew part of what Michael was going through. First Zoe's Internet problems, then my accident and legal troubles, the dance camp disaster, Christopher getting in a fight, and now the career he loved was on the line because of me. It wasn't fair.

And there wasn't a thing I could do to help.

I mulled Kara's words over all day while I filled the kiln with a new layer of glass. Making jewelry kept me grounded, my mind briefly on something other than our problems. I'd spent a lot of hours in the studio lately. Most of my sales for the year came before the holidays. There were my regular clients who'd collected my pieces for years, a couple of jewelry stores in the area kept my stock on hand, and I made the round of craft shows leading up to Christmas.

She had given me good counsel. Michael deserved my support and respect. I would talk things over with him, and we'd decide what to do together.

He had to work that evening, which was a shame because he hated missing home football games. Happy to be finished with my volunteer hours in the refreshment booth, I sat with Kara and Eric, who tactfully didn't bring up the Graitney giant in the room.

I relished the break from worrying about my own problems. Watching the Kickers do their stand dances, and performing to the school's fight song each time the team scored, made the games fly by. Most of all, I loved watching Zoe dance during the halftime show. The girl was a born performer. Christopher, too, in his own way. He and the other Honor Guard members hammed it up, keeping the crowd entertained and cheering for the Giants. Not too hard with their great season. Much to everyone's relief, the loss of the three football players caught drunk driving didn't seem to be impacting the football team.

My respite ended with the halftime show. I walked to the concession stand to get a Diet Coke. It might have been my imagination, but it felt like everyone was watching me, then quickly looking away when I turned their direction. The Blondes, as usual, didn't hide the fact they were whispering together and laughing as I passed. Kuddles and Aimée shot me hate-filled looks. Poor Jennifer smiled weakly. I was being paranoid. Even in a small town, people had things to talk about other than the McKenzie family's problems. Still, it was nice to sit down beside Kara and Eric again. At least, they always had my back.

After the game, the kids went to a victory dance in the school gym. Michael had texted that morning and said he'd like to have dinner with me even though it would be late.

Before the game, I'd whipped up his favorite meal. Once home, I put on a classical Jazz station and tossed together a spinach and mandarin orange salad.

Michael looked drained when he came in, but his eyes lifted in a smile when he saw the dining room table set with our wedding china and candles. The smell of baking lasagna and garlic bread filled the kitchen.

"Wow, it smells good in here." He looped an arm around my back and pulled me into a hard hug and an even more insistent kiss. When we broke apart, I stumbled a little before regaining my footing.

"If I knew lasagna could do that, we'd have it more often," I said with a laugh but meant it.

He grinned ruefully. "I've been a bear lately, She-Girl, and I'm sorry. There's just lots of stuff going on right now."

Michael dumped his keys, phone, and even his service gun on the counter – unusual for him – then washed his hands. I debated telling him I knew what was on his mind but decided he'd take it better after he'd eaten. He wouldn't like what I'd decided to do.

I filled him in on the game while we poured drinks and put the food on the table. Michael started wolfing down the pasta the moment we'd finished praying over the food. It made me happy to see him eat. He'd missed so many meals recently. In no time, he wiped the last drips of marinara sauce from his third slice of lasagna off his plate with a piece of garlic bread, and stretched back in his chair.

"Okay, spill it," he said.

"Spill what?" I tried to look innocent. It was tough keeping anything hidden from a natural-born detective.

"You know what happened with the Mayor, and you've got a scheme cooked up. I can tell."

I'd hoped to make it through mint chocolate-chip ice cream before facing this. I shoved my nearly-full plate of food aside and propped my elbows on the table. "Okay, hear me out first, please."

Michael crossed his thickly corded arms, the happy light that had been in his eyes dimmed.

I rushed on. "Look, you wouldn't be in this mess except for me. Samuel Hardy has no idea when we will know if I'm going to be indicted. He said it could be imminent or take another six months, maybe longer. This whole thing is just hanging over our heads like a guillotine. Now, it's hurting your job. Wouldn't it be better for you and the whole family if I move away? At least until we know what's going to happen. Without me around, your reputation wouldn't be drug through the mud."

Despite all my good intentions earlier, I couldn't help myself. The only way I could see to fix things was to get away. I was the problem.

"Move away?" His eyes narrowed, his voice turned icy

calm. "Where?"

"Aunt Trudy's. She's got that huge house and is thrilled about the idea of our comi—"

Ice shards now formed on his every word. "We? Who...is...we?"

"The kids of course." Instead of growing calmer like Michael did when things got tense, my speech grew quick, high-pitched, and agitated. "Zoe, at least. Because obviously what's happened with her at the hotel in Houston can't be good for your job either, if it gets out. Which it totally may now that the other Kicker girls are in trouble. I thought we could give Christopher the choice. None of this is his fault, and it is his senior year. He may not want—"

"Stop," Michael said softly, but the word slammed into the room like a billy club. "Not a word. I don't want to hear another word about this."

"But it's a good idea. It won't be forever. Well, it could be if I end up in the slammer, but then I guess Zo would *have* to move back with you, but for the—"

He leapt up. The crash as his chair fell over made me jump and finally shut up. Michael took a deep breath. A muscle twitched in his clenched jaw.

He bent over and picked up the chair, carefully placing it back at the table. Then his gaze turned on me. From my seated position, his 6'2" looked even more imposing than usual. My insides quavered, and I pressed back in the seat as far as I could. Not scared, just wishing I could melt away.

"This is not a conversation we are having. Ever." His cool, calm tone stood at odds with the anger I knew surged through him. "We McKenzies are a family, and we face things as a family. No matter what."

He sighed and his countenance softened. "Got it?"

I nodded.

"Good." Michael sat back down. "And for your information, the mayor is caving from pressure from some of his largest donors, parents who are unhappy about their children being arrested for DUI."

Whatever I'd been about to say evaporated. My eyes widened.

"They are pressuring the mayor, as are their friends who do whatever they say."

"So, it's not my fault?"

Michael now sounded weary. "She-Girl, as hard as it is to believe, not everything revolves around you."

I bit my lip feeling like a fool.

Before I could say anything, he continued, "Why don't you go take a bath? Relax a little. The food was delicious and I appreciate it. I'll clean up the dishes."

Maybe our marriage was doing better than I thought. There's not much sexier than a man doing dishes.

Chapter Thirty-Six

Grace

The NEST gathered for its annual retreat at a Christian camp nestled on the end of a beautiful peninsula on Lake Lewisville. The setting of grassy fields and wooded areas felt far removed from the Metroplex, which an undeveloped-bay hid from sight. We always stayed in the Happiness cabin, one of the dozen that ringed the water.

The weekend began with us playing a silly break-the-ice relay game in the large center area of the cabin, which also held two bunkhouse-style rooms for sleeping. I tried to enjoy the fun but had trouble concentrating. The lawyer's call saying the lab results could come back soon, along with the mayor's decision to replace Michael, and the uncertainty over Zoe's pictures continued to crowd my mind.

After dinner in the camp's communal dining room, we gathered back in the cabin. Gabby liked to surprise us with each year's theme. This year's theme seemed chosen specifically for me – God's Peace. We sang worship songs and heard a short message on Isaiah 26:3 "You will keep in perfect peace all who trust in you, all whose thoughts are fixed on you!"

Then we broke apart to begin our silent time with God. Everyone filed outdoors, each woman going her separate way.

The sun cast long shadows over the grass, and the trees darkened into lollipop shapes as I made my way down to the shore. Most of the ladies headed to the other side of camp where there were benches near three big crosses making a dramatic impact highlighted against the lake. But I felt a driving need to be completely alone. I wandered in the opposite direction around a cluster of rocks and willow trees.

It felt great to be outside after the long hot Texas summer. The day had been perfect, in the low 70's. Now the air cooled rapidly carrying the delicious perfume of freshly mown grass. The sudden stillness of a peaceful evening made it seem like there was no one else in the world.

Trying to calm my mind and enter into the silence, I concentrated on my surroundings. Retreats used to be about a break from the busyness of life with two teenagers. Now, when I faced a future locked away from my family – a family I tore apart by my own sin – I craved this time with God.

I hadn't realized how much.

I'd been trying to cope with life on my own and failed miserably. Something about being outside helped God feel closer than he had in a long time.

A desperate need overwhelmed me, far more than a physical thirst or hunger, and I finally understood what Jesus meant when he said we're blessed when we hunger and thirst for righteousness.

I got that now. I understood having no righteousness of my own. Since the time I'd accepted Christ as a twelve-year-old child, I knew that every person ever born messes up, makes mistakes, hurts people, lies, steals, hates in their hearts, and sins in thousands of ways. We've cut ourselves off from a holy God. No one is good. Only Jesus – fully God and fully man – has lived a perfect life. He did what we are incapable of doing.

That's why he alone can be our Savior.

I've known that all my life it seemed. So how could I so badly disappoint him who I proclaim to serve and my family whom I love more than life itself? I didn't have an answer.

I only knew if God didn't come through for me now,

nothing else mattered. I'd spent too much of the last few months giving way to panic and worry, which is sin.

Besides, it did no good.

I'd been all about me for a long time, and I didn't want to live that way any longer. I begged God's forgiveness. I craved peace.

Standing on the rocky shore, I looked and listened hard as the sky darkened from light to dusky blue. As if tired, the sun sank gratefully into soft bands of cloud stripping the horizon like fluffy bed linens in glowing layers of peach, orange, and copper. The lake shone with a mirrored reflection of the sky.

I heard a caw, then a rustle of leaves. A black dart soared overhead where the setting sun silvered an airliner. The rhythmic croaks and chirps of frogs and crickets underscored the piercing quiet. A fish leapt into the air with a wet plop, leaving only expanding rings rippling the smooth surface of the water. Each detail planned and overseen by the Creator who loved me with an everlasting love.

How long had it been since I'd been anyplace so restful? I stood letting the beauty soak in. The sky grew darker, and I felt the earth let out a sigh, settling down for the night after a very long day.

The flaming bands of changing color held my rapt attention until suddenly the first star popped out overhead.

I craned my head back and spotted another. And another. Then too many to count.

Peace washed over my soul as gently as the molten-bronze water shushing against the shore. A sense of the vastness of the universe and the God who holds it in the palm of his hand left me feeling infinitesimally small but incredibly protected and loved, as well.

The calm and security I could not attain on my own settled over me as gently as the night settling over the countryside.

I finally knew, without any doubt whatsoever, that no matter what happened, I'd be all right. Zoe would be all right. Our family would be all right. Even if I went to jail and Zo's pictures appeared online. I had no idea how, but God knew.

And that's all that mattered.

I realized what I'd known all along but let fear obscure. When it comes right down to it, being a Christian means we've given up the right to our own lives because Christ paid for all our mistakes and messes with his own sinless life. If the creator of this painfully beautiful universe did that for us, then we can trust him with everything.

I could trust him.

No matter what.

The essence of faith.

God kept the stars spinning in their courses. He could handle whatever came my way. A sudden image of a glowing lion came to mind. God had everything in hand from the very beginning. Didn't I see the Lion of Judah my first night in the hospital? The invisible band crushing the life out of me for so long loosened. I threw out my arms and spun for joy, like Zoe loved to do when she was a little girl.

When I stopped twirling, I faced the opposite way. While I'd been looking the other direction, the full moon had risen behind me. A silver ribbon glittered across the water to the east like a pathway of light shining all the way to heaven.

A celestial walkway. The way seemed so clear now. I laughed out loud.

Praise music carried to me on the night air, signaling time to return to the cabin. I sent up a grateful prayer of thanksgiving and headed inside.

Chapter Thirty-Seven

Got Him!

The profound peace God blessed me with during the silent retreat remained with me when I got back home and plunged into the frenzy of ordinary life. Michael might be the best of men, but when I'm away from home, I always return to a house in shambles. My heart was so light I didn't care. Like Gabby says, "We can even clean toilets to the glory of God."

I hummed praise songs Monday evening as I went about restoring order.

"Mom! Mo-o-o-m!!"

Zoe hadn't screamed at me with such urgency since one of the strays she'd brought home had puppies in the crawlspace under the staircase. I dropped the armload of damp towels and hurtled down the stairs. We nearly collided at the bottom. A riot of dark curls framed her face. A wild light lit her eyes.

"Whoa!" I stopped her flight with hands on her shoulders. "What happened?"

She looked flushed, almost like she had a fever. Michael followed a few steps behind her. He wore his cop face, but a matching fierce light shone in his eyes.

Zoe jutted her chin up. "We got him, Mom. I figured it out."

My gaze flew to Michael's. "You've got him? You've arrested that pervert?"

He gave a quick shake of his head. "No, but based on Zo's information, the FBI is obtaining a warrant this very moment."

A grim smile flitted across his face. "She did it, She-Girl." He rumpled Zoe's hair. "She broke the case wide open."

Thoughts dashed in and out of my mind. I spun my daughter around and herded her towards the kitchen.

"I want to hear every detail. Who is it? How did you figure it out?"

"Any chance you could whip up an omelette or something while we talk?" Michael asked. "I'm starved."

There were so few times he'd been interested in eating since this whole horrible ordeal started.

"I'd love to." I began rooting for things in the fridge.

Both Michael and Zoe grabbed sodas and sat at the table watching me.

I turned around and looked at them. "I'm not cooking until you guys start talking. Who is it? Tell me everything." I smacked the skillet onto the stove.

"You know him, Mom."

I swung around. "I know him? Someone we *know* did this horrible thing?" The pan was in my hand again held aloft like a weapon.

"You know *of* him," Michael said. "On the dark web, he went by Chase Reynard, but in this part of the world he's known as Rex J. Fowler."

I gasped and nearly dropped the skillet. "The Dallas Channel 7 News roving reporter?"

Both my husband and my daughter nodded, looking furious.

"How did you figure that out?" I turned back around, banged the skillet back down, grabbed a bowl, and started cracking eggs into a bowl with a vengeance.

"Remember that Fun Run we did in middle school to raise money for the school's Booster Club?"

It had been a noble effort, but Zoe and her dancer friends looked more like prancing ballerinas than serious runners. Still, the money went for a good cause.

"Of course, I remember."

"Well in one of the photos, I recognized this super

quiet kid, Jamison Clark, from my school. He runs cross country. Something about seeing him made me remember that run and that Channel 7 News covered the story.

Butter sizzled as, I turned around. "That's right. You girls were all hoping to get your pictures on TV. He interviewed students all day."

Her voice sounded bitter. "Maybe that's why I remember it so well. Rex J. Fowler, Channel 7 News," she said in a mocking news-anchor voice, "took tons of video. Sort of ridiculous for a small-town fund raiser if you think about it."

"Not ridiculous if you're getting pictures of athletic children." The anger in Michael's voice could have cooked the eggs. "Her hunch felt right, so I checked with the boy who originally came forward. Fowler filmed him during a band competition. It was like dominoes. The pieces just fell into place. Every kid we've identified so far has been interviewed by Fowler."

"That's sick. Just sick." I beat the broken eggs. The sight of the stringy gelatinous whites refusing to mix was disgusting. I beat harder.

I'd always been something of a news junky – though, like so many people, I no longer accepted everything I heard or read as true. Still, I liked to think our local media market was not as tainted as the national one where so many famous names had fallen from grace and real news had been replaced by a political agenda. Fowler used his local fame and status to earn parents' and kids' trust.

Could anything be more loathsome? It felt like another personal assault.

Steam rose from the pan when I poured the eggs into the hot skillet. I'd missed some of what Michael had been telling me, too focused on my own thoughts of what I'd like to do to the toothy, smiling, news anchor.

"...enough evidence to get a warrant. They expect to execute it in a couple of hours."

"But I don't understand, why was a reporter shooting video?" I asked interrupting.

Zoe answered. "It turns out that it's not like you see on TV shows. Normally, there isn't a van full of people zipping around. General assignment reporters like Rex J. Fowler, Channel 7 News, are usually one-man bands." Each time she said his name, she mocked an anchor voice. "They shoot, write, edit their own videos. Even when he did have videographers along, they were his buddies, and they were used to him wanting extra takes."

"A nice little set-up," Michael said, grimly. "Not a word of this to anyone, of course."

Zoe gave a mirthless laugh. "I've kept quiet this long. It's not as if I'm suddenly going to go spilling my most shameful secret to the world."

I sprinkled cubed ham and cheddar cheese on the eggs,

hating to ask the question I had to ask. "Do we know any more about Zoe's pictures?"

She answered again, "No. Not yet. When the feds get Rex J. Fowler, Channel 7 News' personal computer, they may learn more."

"The cyber experts have tracked some of the activity from the computer we already found." Michael's voice had a forced, cheerful quality, but I didn't think it fooled either of us. "No news is good news."

"So, we wait. Again." I added avocado slices, then folded the large omelette in half before sliding it onto a platter.

I put it on the table along with salsa and sour cream. Michael took two-thirds and wolfed down every bite. Zoe ate most of the rest. They went through a pile of toast. I had no appetite, even though being alone in the house I'd only eaten yogurt for dinner. Michael and Zoe acted like a burden had been lifted, but to me it felt as if I waited for another phone call in the dark of night. Why, I wasn't sure. Perhaps because Michael's job was still up in the air.

The mayor had given Michael until the end of the year to vacate the office. He had already started putting out feelers about new jobs. Two former Air Force military buddies, now on civilian police forces, had shown real interest. Gratifying. But we hated the thought of moving.

Wouldn't Michael's figuring out who this sextortionist

was help save his job? I shook my head. Since when had the world behaved rationally?

Zoe's long shower threatened to drain the hot water tank when Michael's phone buzzed later that evening. I hoped she left me some water, although no amount of scrubbing would remove the filth that newsman had brought into our lives. Michael glanced at the phone screen and jumped up.

"Bingo." He strode across the room and gave me a kiss. "Here we go."

There was no sense in asking him where he was going. "Be safe."

He turned at the doorway and winked. "Watch for breaking news at ten."

Chapter Thirty-Eight

Breaking News

The arrest and perp walk of Rex J. Fowler Channel 7 News was all anyone could talk about the next day. That afternoon so many moms stayed during dance class it was standing room only, but no one seemed to mind.

"Even Channel 7 is covering the story at the top of the broadcast," Dolores said, shaking her head.

"Well, it *is* child porn," another mom said dropping her voice on the last word, even though there was no way the kids could hear us over the music Rochelle had cranked.

"I can't believe he got away with it for so long," Kara said. "Fowler's been at that station ever since I moved here. That was more than twenty years ago."

"He's probably filmed all our kids, even L&O," put in Ida with a dramatic shiver. "The thought gives me the creeps."

Kara looked around the group, catching a few eyes. "Remember when our girls did that run to raise money for the Booster Club in middle school?"

My insides swooshed away.

"He interviewed several of our girls," she went on. "I remember because Emily was hoping she'd get on TV. They didn't use her footage, but what if that pervert still has pictures of our girls? The news said he was being indicted not only for having kiddy...you-know-what, but for blackmailing local children. What if any of them are kids we know? Can you imagine anything worse?"

Kara stared at the other moms. They all stared back, horror on their faces as this thought sank in. I tried to keep my own face neutral and wished I hadn't gotten all my errands run so I could stay and talk. I'm not the world's best at hiding my thoughts. Thankfully the other moms were so wrapped up in every little detail of the story that had leaked to the press, they paid no attention to me sitting there feeling uncomfortable.

Not that it was all bad.

A perverse part of me took great pleasure that Rex J. Fowler's spectacular downfall from celebrity to vile predator topped every newspaper and began every news broadcast for the next week. People waiting in line at the bank, grocery store, and library could talk of nothing else.

He deserved every single bit of bad press. Still, each time his name came up, I feared Zoe's would follow.

Thank God, the law protects the names of minors. But of course, that wouldn't stop the rumor mill. I was grateful every day that Zoe's name wasn't out there, but now this was such a huge news story, reporters would be digging into it. The likelihood of her exposure seemed to have gone up exponentially. I hadn't dreamed catching the perpetrator would be such a two-edged sword.

Still, it gave me a fresh chance every morning to trust God with this latest issue. I was done with worrying. The Bible said God would carry all our burdens. I was determined to let him.

I got another chance sooner than expected.

Chapter Thirty-Nine

The Results Are In

When I turned the phone back on after working in the studio all afternoon, there was a message from the lawyer's office. The results of my tox screen were back. His assistant said I needed to schedule an appointment with the attorney to learn what the tests showed and to decide where to go from there.

"Where to go from there?" It sounded ominous.

I did my best for the next day and a half not to think what those words might portend. Since committing to trusting God, I seemed to be getting lots of practice at it.

Michael held my hand as the receptionist led us down a long hallway to Samuel Hardy's office, our footsteps muted by the plush carpet. His door stood open, and he looked up with a smile when she announced us. That felt like a good sign.

We sat in a pair of modern leather chairs facing his broad desk with a view of the Dallas skyline behind. Criminal defense attorneys obviously made good money. For the first time, I wondered how we could afford his services. An installment plan I hoped.

He glanced down at some papers and then looked up at us, the smile gone.

I gave Michael's hand a nervous squeeze. The peace God had given me about the entire situation remained, but that didn't mean I was eager to hear my fate.

"We've received the report from the state forensics lab."

He handed us a copy and read it out loud. Michael nodded along. I felt totally lost and simply stared at the attorney for a long moment when he'd finished.

"So, does this means that neither alcohol nor drugs had anything to do with the accident?" I asked, certain I'd misunderstood.

"That's correct. The emesis evidence collected from the clothing you wore at the scene and subsequent blood work show unequivocally that you had only a trace amount of alcohol and no drugs, other than acceptable levels of cold meds, in your system. Since the stomach contents were under your blood stains, forensics determined that you vomited first, which caused you to pass out. Most likely the result of a sudden drop in blood pressure. Then you crashed the car. After reading your medical records and consulting with your doctors, I learned that all this was attributable to a severe bleeding ulcer."

He sent me a kindly smile. "Your BAC, blood alcohol content, was less than .02 and by no means impaired your functioning. There isn't a prosecutor alive who would try to take that to court."

"The bleeding ulcer made her throw up and pass out, which caused the collision," Michael restated in his get-everything-by-the-book tone. "There was no way for Sheena to have avoided the accident."

"I've been informed by experts that with bleeding ulcers symptoms can strike quickly. In Mrs. McKenzie's case, her being ill with the sinus infection masked the first signs of something more serious being wrong."

I remembered the sharp-knife pains in my gut, which I thought were due to a nasty bug that had me stuffy and coughing.

Somewhere in the recesses of my mind an angel chorus sang. Tracy certainly danced along. Could it possibly be true that not only was I not guilty, but I couldn't even have prevented the accident?

"What happens now legally?" I finally managed to ask.

"Legally, the state is not filing charges. The accident

was simply that, a tragic accident."

"She's criminally cleared," Michael said calmly, "but what about a civil suit since technically she was at fault?"

I'd been so worried about going to jail, I never once thought about someone suing me.

Hardy grinned at my husband. "You carry an unusually generous umbrella policy on top of your regular insurance."

"People like to sue cops," Michael said.

"Tracy Cumming's estate stated they have no interest in suing. Your insurance adequately covered the expenses of the family in the other vehicle. I've spoken with both attorneys, and they are accepting what's already been paid as full settlement for any damages."

He handed me another packet of papers. "Here is the documentation."

"And where do we go from here?'" I asked.

Hardy looked puzzled for a split second then comprehension dawned. "Ah, yes. my assistant's stock phraseology. We don't often have clients whose BAC reports come back negative. You are completely free and clear."

A cool river of relief washed over me.

Thank goodness Michael was there to say all the proper things. After I heard those words, everything was a blur. My mind couldn't seem to shift gears so quickly. I'd finally come to a sense of peace with God being in control of whatever happened, even if that meant a lengthy trial and jail time. Then, in only a matter of minutes, I found out the whole nightmare was behind me.

Of course, the gaping hole Tracy left in my life and the lives of everyone else who loved her would never be gone.

Days ago, I'd have thought hearing this news would have lifted the sense of guilt I'd been struggling with for months, but I realized with a jolt that even before we entered Samuel Hardy's office, the guilt had been gone. I tried to explain it to Michael on the drive home.

"It's great news for the family that we don't have to deal with the mess this could have been, but God already granted me peace, no matter what happens."

He cast me a quick look. "You did some business with Jesus during your silent retreat, didn't you? You've seemed different since you've been home. Calmer."

One of the things I love about Michael is that he doesn't miss anything.

"Still, you must feel great not to be at fault," he added.

I turned in my seat toward him. "But I still *am* at fault. Maybe not for the accident or Tracy's death. But I still did something wrong. For years, we've told the kids to never get in the car with someone whose been drinking, even if they've only had one drink. It's not worth it. Call for a ride. But I broke our own rule. I didn't sin because I had a couple of drinks, but I was in the wrong by not being a good role model for our kids. For not doing what we tell them to do."

"None of us is a perfect parent, She-Girl." He reached over and put a hand on my leg. The bandage was long gone, but the jagged scar would always be a reminder of a tough time and God's miraculous intervention.

"Granted," I agreed. "I just blew it in spectacular fashion, especially by staying mad at God for so long and wrongly thinking he was mad at me."

"True, but at least you can relate to what Zoe's been going through."

"There's that."

I couldn't wait for the kids to come home from school to give them the good news. Michael went to work and I hit the grocery store. We needed to celebrate. The miraculous end to one of our problems called for our family's favorite food – Mexican. I grilled both chicken and steak as well as onions and Poblano peppers for fajitas. Fresh pico de gallo, queso, and guacamole, along with roasted corn-on-the-cob, would round out our feast.

The dining room table looked festive with bright orange placemats decorated with red, green, and yellow chili-peppers. I'd just put down a chip-and-dip bowl shaped like a Sombrero when I heard the door open. I assumed it was the kids coming in from High Kicker and soccer practice.

"Hi, honey," Michael shouted from the kitchen, "I'm home."

It made me laugh. He hadn't done that in years. As newlyweds, we'd called that out to one another whenever we entered the house. When had we quit doing so?

Just as I turned around, he swooped me up in his arms and twirled me, before setting me back down.

He hadn't looked so happy in months or so carefree. "We have so much to celebrate." Michael gave me a quick kiss.

A grin still curled my lips when the kids clattered into the kitchen a short time later.

"I'm starved," Christopher said, his nose twitching. "It smells great in here."

"Me, too." Zoe picked a piece of golden sautéed onion out of the frying pan.

I swatted at her hand. "Go wash up. We're eating in the other room."

Michael carried things to the table, while I lit a few colorful votive candles. After saying grace, we ate and filled the kids in on what the lawyer had said.

The guys were on their third platefuls, the eating not stopping the excited chatter, when Michael paused to read a text. He frowned for a moment, and I watched him scroll back to the top and reread. God's got it, I reminded myself instead of worrying something bad was in the works. Zoe and Christopher were hotly debating whether orange or white queso was better, when Michael's gaze caught and held mine.

I tried to read his expression. *Incredulous* was the only word I could come up with.

"I'll be right back," he said, scooting the chair back. "I've got to make a quick call."

The kids didn't seem to notice a thing, but the chips and pico I ate mindlessly could have been cardboard. In no time, he came back and stood with his hands on the back of the chair.

"We are the most blessed family in the entire world," he announced.

This got the kids' attention. Michael wasn't given to hyperbole. We all looked at him waiting for his next words. Something had to be up. We'd already completely discussed the arrest of Rex J. Fowler and my legal exoneration.

How did things get any better?

Michael smiled broadly, drawing out the moment. "I've just gotten off the phone with Jerry Samuel, lead FBI agent on the Fowler investigation." Again, he paused and looked at each one of us in turn, ending with his gaze resting on his daughter. "Zoe, you're in the clear."

She gave a sharp intake of breath and her hand flew to her mouth.

"What?" I asked. "What does that mean, 'in the clear?'"

Joy radiated off him. "Her pictures never went online, and they never will."

Zo and I screamed and jumped up at the same time. I hugged Michael. She hugged Christopher. Then we all bumped together in a great big family hug like we'd done when the kids were little.

We started talking over one another.

Christopher called for order, "Quiet, you guys. Let Dad talk. I want to know how they know this."

We all slid back into our chairs, except for Michael. Clearly too excited to sit, he paced at the end of the table.

"Remember I told you Fowler was unusual because he had pictures of both girls and boys."

"Eww," Zoe said. "That's so sick."

Christopher made a face and shook his head in disgust.

"Turns out he had a reason. He traded the pictures of boys with other pedophiles, but he kept his girl pictures as a private stash. Those pictures are in entirely separate files for his eyes only. They never were online."

"How can you be sure?" I demanded. "Maybe the FBI just hasn't been able to find them yet."

"Nope. They were never on the Internet. As part of his plea bargain, Fowler confirmed the information."

Zoe's voice sounded small, "What will happen to…those pictures?"

"The devices with the girls' images will be locked up in evidence storage, never to be seen again. Jerry told me that Fowler wants to avoid the publicity of a trial, so he's pled guilty."

Michael smiled triumphant. "He's going away for a very long time."

Chapter Forty

Confess At The Nest

Only God could have orchestrated such wonderful outcomes. Never in our wildest imaginations could Zoe and my problems have been resolved so perfectly, which was good because life is still life. The good news about Zoe's pictures helped her weather her disappointment in Izzy's landing the solo if the football team made it to the final playoff, which looked like a sure thing.

"Honestly, Izzy," I overheard her saying to her friend as she walked into the family room, phone pressed to her ear, "if it had to be someone else, I wanted it to be you or Em. You'll do great. You should be the one to dance, since you're our Captain."

The girls had used the large deck around the pool to work on their routines. I'd handled cheerleading and snacks. They'd all looked great to me.

I muted the home improvement show I'd been watching, Andy draped over my lap. His claws opened and closed in kitty-contentment as I ran my fingernails down his back.

Zoe got off the phone and plopped down beside me.

"Are you really okay about not getting the solo?"

"Not going to lie," she said scooching down and putting her stocking feet up on the coffee table. "I'll be jealous. Can you imagine dancing at Jerry World? It holds like 100,000 people."

I laughed. "I don't think quite that many will be there for the high school 4A Championship game."

"I know. And it's not like I won't be dancing." She picked up Andy who'd left my lap to greet her. Fickle feline.

"The Kickers have the most awesome routine. We're doing the whole Rockettes' style high kick thing. It will be incredible, especially on those massive screens."

Cowboy stadium had high definition video screens that stretched from 20-yard line to 20-yard line.

"And the solo is only about a minute and a half out of a five-minute song. Still..." her voice sounded wistful. She looked at me. "I am glad Izzy got it. She's had a rough year."

Zoe's empathy amazed me. I hadn't given it a

moment's thought, but she was right. Isabella had been friends with Layla and Madison forever. It must be hard on her to see them disgraced and no longer part of the dance team.

I put an arm around her shoulder.

"Hey, would you do me a favor?" I asked.

"Sure, Mom. What is it?"

"Could you come to the NEST with me tonight? It's time I came clean to my closest friends, and I could use the moral support."

It was her turn to look surprised at me. "Of course, can I bring Em?"

I called Gabby and gave her a heads-up. She must have gotten word out that it would be a special evening, because every single Chick showed up. Some of the ladies sat two rows deep, spilling into the dining room.

After we finished the opening praise songs, Gabby turned to me with an encouraging smile. "Sheena, you have something you want to share with us?"

Words failed me for a moment. I looked around the circle of familiar women, each with a history tied to my own. For months, one of my hugest fears had been seeing disappointment on their faces. Seeing disgust. Judgment.

But the Bible says we are to confess our sins one to another. It also says God comforts us so we can comfort others with the same help God gives us. Perhaps one of my friends needed to hear my story.

I took a deep breath and began with the good news. "I'm still trying to wrap my mind around what I've learned recently. Michael told me all this right after the accident, and you all probably know it, but my mind was a mess for a while, so I couldn't remember much. Anyway, everyone says it's a miracle I'm alive, but…it really is. It's an absolute miracle! I know all of you praying for me helped.

"Michael said when he got the call about me being airlifted to the hospital and they told him the state I was in, he thought he was going there to pick up my body." I stopped and took a hasty slurp of water, swallowing with a constricted throat.

"My blood pressure was so low it caused me to be hypoxic. The lack of oxygen sent me into organ failure. I didn't have measurable blood pressure, oxygen, or even a heartbeat for a while. There is literally no reason I should be alive or not have severe brain damage."

Gabby spoke up. "I know a reason why. A gracious God and the prayers of the saints."

"That is completely true, but there's something I haven't told you all, and I need to confess. I should have done so a long time ago, but I was foolishly hiding my sin because I was afraid of losing your approval." I paused, getting my nerve up. No one seemed to breath. "Tracy and I had drinks earlier that evening. Since I can't remember anything about that night, I've worried for months that my drinking caused the accident. I thought it was my fault that Tracy is dead."

Several women let out compassionate little murmurs.

"However, the test results have come back, and yesterday I went over everything with my doctor. Alcohol may have exacerbated my dehydration, but there was nearly none in my system at the time of the accident. Nowhere near the legal limit. I actually passed out right before the crash from a drop in blood pressure caused by a bleeding ulcer."

Everyone's gaze drilled into me.

"It was all a horrible accident. Still, I've had to deal with the guilt and shame that I lived and Tracy died, no matter how it came about. But I was still at fault. I was in the wrong to have broken a rule we'd laid down for our kids. Never drive after even one drink."

There were ladies nodding along with my words. I saw misty eyes. They all loved Tracy, too.

"I'll never have an answer to why I lived and Tracy didn't, but I know that God promises to make good come from even the worst situations." I pressed my lips together against the catch in my throat, took a breath, and went on.

"However, there is something I've learned from all this. God doesn't just forgive our sins before we are saved. He's a God of second chances, and third chances, and fourth, and as many as we need. His love is that wonderful. We don't earn his love in the first place, and we can't lose it by what we do later. He forgave me long before I learned to forgive myself."

I laughed a little, which broke the tension in the room. "Not that the Bible says anything about forgiving ourselves. When we confess our sins, God is faithful to forgive us and cleanse us of all unrighteousness. There's nothing else for us to do but stand on that truth. And that's why I'm telling you all this tonight."

Zoe sat with Emily on the couch beside Kara. The two girls were holding hands. Tears ran down Emily's cheeks.

Gabby said, "What a practical lesson that our identity is not in what we *do,* as the enemy would have us believe when he points to our failures. Rather, God says our identity is in *who* we are, which is his through Christ. Our *who* not our *do*. It's all about relationship. About his grace."

My next words were especially for my daughter. "That's right. I get it now. Since God says there is no condemnation for those in Christ Jesus, it means no guilt, no shame. No matter how we feel."

We'd discussed this for a long time a few days ago,

and I think she finally got it. Me, too. She nodded, and tears welled up in my own eyes.

Happy tears.

Chapter Forty-One

Petition

Kara told me Eric wanted to publish a short piece about the car crash exonerating me, since such ugly rumors had been floating around town for so long. I told her to thank him, but that he didn't need to do it for my sake. I'd learned that people will do, say, and believe what they want, and I was okay with that. I didn't need everyone's approval any longer.

My real friends and family had stood by me when I needed them, and that was good enough for me.

Eric did it anyway.

Once again, Michael was sitting at the table when his phone chirped, just having finished reading the not so little article. This time he'd eaten a hearty breakfast of hash browns, bacon, and eggs. Since the arrest of Rex J. Fowler

Channel 7 News, his appetite had returned. He'd laughingly told me it was a good thing he and Christopher had started lifting weights again or he'd lose his manly physique.

His sense of humor was back, too.

Early morning sunshine lit the table, falling on the cornucopia centerpiece left over from Thanksgiving. Michael pulled out his phone and eyed the text. At the same time, my phone rang. I answered. It was Kara.

"Has Michael seen the news yet?"

"The article? It was wonderful. Eric didn't need to do all that."

"No. The new news."

"What new news?" I asked her, looking at Michael.

He shook his head as a look of amazement broke across his face. His eyes scanned the phone again.

"I think he just got it," I told her. "Call you back."

"What's up?" I asked my stunned-looking husband.

"Our illustrious mayor has changed his mind about my termination."

"Changed his mind? Why?"

"Seems the publisher of our newspaper started a petition to keep me in office. It's already garnered the signature of over fifty-three percent of the city's registered voters, and it's only been circulating for four days."

I had a feeling my darling Kara had a little something

to do with prompting her husband to start the petition.

"Those are not numbers," I said in an announcer's voice, "that The Honorable Alfred Waverly, Mayor of Graitney, Texas would like to run up against next election."

Michael beamed. "10-4."

Chapter Forty-Two

A Jolly Giant Christmas

Three weeks later

The whole town had gone Giant nuts. Everyone joked that there were more Giant Joe green and white banners around town than Christmas decorations. For the first time in its history, Graitney High School was going to be in the final playoff game for the state Class 4A Division II championship. The Giants were going head to head with the Bott's Creek Hawks.

My kids were stoked: Christopher because as a senior Honor Guard member he'd be going out in a blaze of glory, and Zoe because her dream of dancing in the huge stadium where the Texas Cowboys played was coming true. Everyone in town seemed to be going to the game the Saturday before Christmas. The town hired several charter buses to take those who didn't want to drive.

Dolores's husband played Santa during the "Lighting of the Square" event in Graitney each year. She told me most of the kiddos hadn't asked for presents but for a Giants' win. Football fandom starts young in Texas.

Thankfully, most people could look forward to the game with excitement, innocent of the online threats Michael and his officers had to cope with.

"We assume it's just some teen acting out with the anonymity of the Internet. Probably a case of jealousy gone too far," he told me as we wrapped packages late one night after Christopher and Zoe had gone to sleep. "But in today's world with school shootings and pipe bombings, we have to take each threat seriously."

"But your department isn't responsible for security at the game, is it?" I had assumed we'd get to watch our kids perform together.

"Not at all. There are event security personnel and Arlington police for that. However, we are responsible for our students and players while they are here at school getting ready and, personally, I'm making sure all the school busses are cleared and safe before the kids even load up."

The reality of what he said so casually hit like the forty-mile-an-hour wind pummeling the house from the first artic cold snap of the season. I shivered, even though we were perfectly warm indoors. The embers of the fire we'd enjoyed earlier glowed a radiant orange amidst heaps of ash.

For a moment, my mind screamed not to let Christopher or Zoe go anywhere near that game. It wasn't worth the risk. But immediately, I took that thought captive and realized that nothing in life was guaranteed safe. I'd learned to trust God this far, I wasn't going to stop now.

"I'm sure Principal Harrison appreciates your efforts," I said in an offhand tone.

Michael grinned. "True. He's nervous as a three-legged goat on a frozen pond over this game as it is. You'd think he was the quarterback."

I chuckled. It was great to have my goofy husband back.

Since the Giants had sailed into the playoffs, I naively thought game day would go off without a hitch. That was before the calls started coming in. Christopher got to school without his black cowboy hat – an essential part of his uniform – and didn't have time to come home and get it. He asked me to run it up to him, something he'd never done in four years of being on the squad. It just showed how wound up and excited everyone was. I raced to school with the missing hat.

I'd no more than gotten in my car again, than Zoe texted. Seems Layla and Madison were in the parking lot wishing the football players good luck before they got on the bus, and they'd said obnoxious things to her in front of everyone.

She was crying in the bathroom.

It didn't take a lot of imagination to figure out what two dethroned teenaged girls might say to someone who they thought had gotten away with the same infraction without any consequences.

"You should have seen Emily light into them." A tinge of pride crept into her voice. "Savage!"

Why did something like this happen today of all days? Zoe deserved something to go right for once this year.

I shot her a commiserating text, sent up a quick prayer, and muttered under my breath as I raced home to grab my stuff before picking up Kara. We were riding together to Arlington. Michael would meet me at the game because he had to wait and make sure everything went smoothly at school first. I'd nearly forgotten about the threats he'd mentioned a few days before. Remembering them knotted my stomach. Off went another popcorn prayer. Good thing God isn't impressed with fancy words or length of our supplications.

Before she jumped into the car, Kara threw enough bags in the back of my CX-5 for a weeklong cruise.

"I've got treats for the Kickers for their ride home after the game," she explained.

"I thought someone was already handling that."

"Yes, but it's Carla, the dentist, and she always gives them healthy snacks. I've got six different flavors of gourmet popcorn."

She slammed the car door. "I bet Zo's flying high as a kite right now," she said shooting me a huge grin. "Although, I do feel bad for poor Izzy."

I gave her a quizzical look before pulling out of the driveway. "Why? What happened to Izzy?"

"You don't know?"

"Obviously," I said rather snappily. How in the world did she manage to know everything before me?

"Jeesh! Don't take my head off."

"Sorry. It's already been a long day and it's only nine-thirty."

The Class 4A Division II game didn't start until three, but we were going to grab lunch somewhere fun and get to the stadium early, probably catching the tail end of an earlier game. We didn't want to miss one minute of the Giants' big event.

"I heard from Jennifer about thirty minutes ago. Poor Izzy slipped on some soap getting out of the shower this morning and sprained her ankle. It's swollen up like a cantaloupe."

"Oh, my gosh. The poor thing. She won't get to dance."

"Right. She won't get to dance." Kara paused.

I was busy pulling onto the freeway. An exodus of cars streamed from our little town for the city.

"So…" she dragged the sentence out, "who is her understudy?"

"Zoe…Zoe! Are you kidding me?" I nearly swerved into the other lane. "Zo gets to dance the solo today?"

"She does!"

"I don't think she knows. Well, she probably knows now. She didn't know about thirty minutes ago because she was crying in the bathroom," I rambled.

"Was it her nervous stomach that had her upset?" Kara asked.

"No, it was something else. Hopefully, she doesn't have time to get nervous. She's probably chair-dancing – going through the routine in her head – like athlete's do. Thinking about the solo is better than what she was worried about before."

We had quite a drive, so I settled down and told Kara about the morning so far. As soon as the kids entered school, it was radio silence. All phones off or the sponsor would have confiscated them. I doubted I could even talk to my daughter before her moment in the spotlight. She had to be so excited.

Unless, she was letting the things Layla and Madison had said get to her. Zo wouldn't do that. She, too, had learned her lesson this year about letting God take care of the details.

And, wow, had he ever!

I'd never been inside the AT&T stadium. It felt like standing in the middle of an enormous football. Rows upon rows of seats rose above the green turf. Kara and I watched the end of the previous game in a nose-bleed section before making our way to better seats. The temperature hovered in the mid-sixties with no chance of rain, so the retractable roof had been slowly opened with everyone snapping pictures of the amazing process.

Eric, who had connections everywhere, could have wrangled us seats in the Founders Club, if this had been a Cowboys' game. They would have been worth a fortune. But as it was the high school playoffs, the box seats weren't open. He got there early enough to snag 50-yard-line seats in the first deck. Also, fabulous. He and Michael met us there.

"Everything go okay at school, I take it?" I said to Michael as he got up to let us into our seats.

"That's affirmative." He winked.

Michael was in a great mood if he was using cop-speak. I'm sure it felt good having the burden of being responsible for the kids' welfare today on someone else's shoulders.

I'd no more had the thought and thanked Eric for saving us wonderful seats than I saw Kuddles Malik and Aimée Alterman marching up the stairs, husbands in tow. They glared as they passed. I took perverse pleasure in noting their seats were a deck higher than ours. It seemed Kuddles, who was always running late, was finally paying for her unrelenting tardiness.

I refused to let thoughts of them ruin the fun of seeing Christopher's last football game as an Honor Guard member. The boys did push-ups equal to the team's points every time they scored. Since in some of the games they'd skunked the other teams by more than fifty points, he said it was the best triceps workout ever invented. Sometimes the cheerleaders stood with booted foot on their backs while they did the push-ups. Christopher loved every minute of it.

Oh, to be young and invincible again.

While we waited, we got sodas and talked about the day and what a win would mean for Graitney. Michael and I were just discussing how excited Zoe must be feeling when the loudspeaker announced the beginning of the game. It might only be the 4A championship, but much of the stadium held screaming fans and other football junkies.

Our yells blended with the others as our mighty Giants, looking rather puny against such a huge backdrop, raced onto the field. The green and white Giants faced the red and gold Hawks. The first half was a nail-bitter. We'd grown used to the Giants dominating, so their going into half time neck and neck – fourteen to fourteen – was unusual.

I have no idea what the Hawks band and dance team did during their fifteen minutes of fame. I simply couldn't concentrate. There was no reason for Zoe to be nervous; I was doing a fine job for her.

The moment the Graitney band came on the field to do their Elton John compilation, my worries escalated. It had been her biggest dream to dance the solo today, but she hadn't expected to. Would she be ready? Had she kept practicing even though Izzy was slotted to do the dance? Another popcorn prayer. Peace returned.

The band filed off the field and the Kickers strutted on. They looked adorable in red dresses cinched at the waist with broad white belts, white cowboy boots, and Santa hats. They formed a kick line to start dancing to a medley of Christmas tunes: "I Saw Mommy Kissing Santa Claus," "Grandma Got Run Over by a Reindeer," and "Rockin' Around a Christmas Tree."

After the silly exuberance, the volume and tone

abruptly changed. Zoe stepped out from the group and began dancing to "I'll Be Home for Christmas."

It felt as if everyone in the huge stadium held their breath, hearts longing for the most important place on earth – home. She danced flawlessly.

Intense pride in the competent young woman Zoe had become filled me to overflowing.

I watched my daughter's face as she finished the short segment, balanced on one foot, the other pointed over her head, arms outstretched, head high. Joy radiated off her like beams of light.

It couldn't get any better than that glorious moment. I seemed to float on the sunbeams pouring through the open ceiling.

A small commotion down below drew my attention away from Zoe. With the Kickers still on the field, Rochelle joined Miss Williams leading a small, elderly woman by the hand.

"Ladies and gentleman, we take a brief pause today before resuming our game," boomed the voice on the loud speakers, "for an important announcement to the good people of Graitney and the many others who have been touched by the life of an extraordinary young woman."

My spine curled.

A person in a stadium uniform handed Miss Williams a microphone.

"Hello, everyone. As those of you from Graitney know, I'm the high school dance troupe sponsor, Marcia Williams. As many of you also know, my cousin, Rochelle Williams is the owner of the *Heart For Dance* studio where most of our team takes lessons."

She paused and looked around, as if just noticing all the people gazing down on her. "This year has been a difficult one for Rochelle as her business partner, mentor, and dear friend, Tracy Cummings, was killed in a tragic car accident."

I felt faint. My head spun. I didn't think I could sit and listen to this, but there was no place to run and hide in the 100,000-person giant fishbowl.

"Tracy was admired not only by me and her students, but by all the citizens of our town. She brought a love and appreciation of the arts to a rather rough and countrified corner of the Metroplex."

Polite chuckles broke out.

"Once again, this amazing woman has managed to touch other people's lives with her own," Miss Williams continued. "Let me turn the microphone over to Tracy's Great Aunt Harriet, the woman who raised her after Tracy's parents were killed in an automobile accident themselves."

She handed the mic to the woman beside her who said in a quavering yet strong voice, "Those of you who knew

my girl will not be surprised in the least to hear that Tracy
was an organ donor. Her organs saved at least seven lives,
and her eyes helped a couple of others." The woman
stopped, her gaze drilling into the faces of those around the
stadium, as if daring anyone to dispute this. No one had
moved since they'd begun talking. "My dear Tracy's
tissues and bones helped dozens more."

Applause drowned her voice.

When it died down, Aunt Harriet continued, "There is
more. Today I'd like to announce the Tracy Cummings
College Scholarship for children who are in the foster care
system." She smiled and laid a hand on Rochelle's arm.
"Our Tracy's parents left her with quite an inheritance.
Even in dying, our dear girl made sure that many
generations of deserving children will get the help they
need to have a better life."

I gripped Michael's hand.

He leaned down and whispered in my ear, "You meant
evil against me, but God meant it for good, to bring it about
that many people should be kept alive, as they are today."

Genesis 50:20. I'd been praying that scripture since I'd
woken up in the hospital hoping God would redeem the
worst thing that had ever happened in my life. Now, it
seemed that he had.

The enemy didn't win that horrible night, after all.

The Giant's trounced the Hawks in the second half, but

my thoughts weren't on the game. As soon as it ended, Michael and I made our way to where Tracy's Aunt Harriet sat.

She turned warm brown eyes on me the moment she spotted us.

Rising, she pulled me into a hug. "Sheena, darling. My fondest wish was to see you today."

Arms around her frail body, I clung to her as if she were Tracy herself.

When we finally broke apart, she continued to grip one of my arms. "You do know that you were my sweet girl's anchor her entire life, don't you?"

I couldn't speak.

"Of anyone in the world she would have wanted with her at the end, it was you, Sheena."

She squeezed my arm. "There isn't a day that goes by that I don't think of something you said that's helped me get through this difficult time."

I had no idea what that could be.

Aunt Harriet's free hand lifted a blue and silver pendant off her chest. One of my earliest creations. "I've always loved this necklace that you gave me years ago, but it's what you told me about the process that's stayed with me.

"You said that it is going through intense heat and fire that turns ordinary glass into a one-of-a-kind piece of art.

Just like God will do with us during trials if we'll let him. If we will just trust him."

She dropped the necklace and her soft hand cupped my cheek. "I've been talking to Miss Williams, Rochelle, and others. After everything that's happened, you've soldiered on, been there for the Kickers, your family, and friends.

"It seems you, my dear, have come through this trial as a beautiful piece of God's handiwork."

Acknowledgments

The author wishes to acknowledge the invaluable assistance of the following people:

Family – Beau, Brenna & Josef, Kyle & Allie, Alex & Alexandra for always supporting my writing.

Writing friends – Brandi Midkiff, Cheryl Crouch, Jackie Stem, Phil Hall, Cindy Wood, Bill & Audette Kincaid, Dale Fidler – all talented writers and gifted critique partners.

Fact checking – George Roland, attorney; Shannon Hartzell, law enforcement; Peggy Nickell, medical; Tonya Littmann, glass jewelry.

Interior and Cover Design – Marji Laine, Roaring Lambs Book Production Services; Amanda Robertson, proofreading.

Any mistakes in the manuscript are entirely the author's.

Questions For Discussion

Which of the main characters did you relate to and why?

The beginning of the book alternates between what was happening to Sheena in the hospital and what had led up to her being there. Did this help you understand how Sheena experienced the things she was going through?

Have you ever felt excluded from a group?

Do adults worry about fitting in as much as teens?

The story is set in a small town. Would it have worked as well if it were set in a big city?

What do the homes of The Blondes and the McKenzies say about their families?

Both the mom and daughter made a series of poor decisions, does this seem realistic? Why or why not?

Sheena was dealing with a brain injury. Did it effect how she responded to the problems in her life?

How should people handle stress? Does this match what they actually do?

Were you surprised on learning what had happened in the accident?

What role does Tracy play in the book?

Sheena tries to pick a fight with her husband because she was upset. Does this happen in marriage?

Sheena wrestles with the feeling that she failed to protect her daughter. Was she at fault for what happened to Zoe?

How much control can parents reasonably expect to have over their teen's lives?

Can you relate to Sheena and Zoe feeling like they've done something unforgivable?

How did they handle the feeling that everything was spinning out of control?

How could they have better handled that experience?

Did Michael's being the chief of police make things more difficult or easier for the family?

Sheena finally came to peace with all that was happening. How did she get there?

Had things already resolved before she came to being at peace?

If not, how was she able to handle uncertainty when she hadn't been able to before?

How did Zoe aiding her father to identify the sextortionist help her deal with what happened to her?

Sheena felt she needed to confess to her friends at the NEST the poor way she'd been dealing with things. How important is it to have a support group when facing difficulties?

Problems continued to come to their family, but Sheena learned to refuse to let her mind dwell on those issues. How did this help her stay at peace?

Sheena called her recovery from her medical issues a miracle. Do you think God works miraculously?

If so, can you give any examples?

Whether you are a person of faith or not, how did you respond to Sheena and Zoe's crisis of faith?

The author chose the analogy of making glass necklaces using heat and fire to demonstrate what happened in Sheena's life. Do you think this is an apt comparison?

About The Author

Mary is a short story writer with a hundred stories in various magazines. These include *Woman's World Magazine, True Story, True Experience, True Romance, True Love, and True Confessions* and others. She has a master's degree in communication and recently finished a year-long course in biblical counseling. She's on the women's mentoring board of a large church. These pursuits helped form the basis of her first book, *Unforgivable*.

A couple of years ago, she suffered a medical issue which resulted in temporary memory loss. The feeling of helplessness when one can't remember what's happened was the springboard for this story.

She and her husband live in North Texas, as do their adult kids and grandkids.

More On Sextortion

Sextortion describes a crime that happens online when an adult convinces a person who is younger than eighteen to share sexual pictures or perform sexual acts on a webcam.

Sad Statistics:

The National Center for Missing and Exploited Children's Cyber Tipline receives reports regarding suspected child sexual exploitation, including "sextortion," a new online exploitation crime directed towards children in which non-physical forms of coercion are used, such as blackmail, to acquire sexual content from the child, engage in sex with the child, or obtain money from the child.

Between October, 2013 and April, 2016, NCMEC received 1,428 reports of sextortion of minors. Seventy-eight percent were female.

Research shows that at least 22% of teenaged girls have posted nude or seminude photos or videos.

Christian families are not exempt from this growing problem.

If you think this may have happened to you, tell a trusted adult. It is not your fault. This is a crime and the perpetrator needs to be caught.

Resources:

Call the FBI at 800-CALL FBI or go to tips.fbi.gov

This website explains the issue:
https://www.fbi.gov/news/stories/stop-sextortion-youth-face-risk-online-090319

Made in the USA
Monee, IL
17 October 2020